FAI VENGEANCE

Carol L. Monfredo

Copyright © 2024 *Carol L. Monfredo*
All Rights Reserved.

This book is subject to the condition that no part of this book is to be reproduced, transmitted in any form or means; electronic or mechanical, stored in a retrieval system, photocopied, recorded, scanned, or otherwise. Any of these actions require the proper written permission of the author.

"You see things; and you say 'why?' But I dream things that never were, and I say 'why not?'"

George Bernard Shaw

To all of my friends who enjoyed my "Historical Romance" writing. I hope to add my first "Romantic Mystery" to your library.

Contents

About the Author   1

Chapter 1   2

Chapter 2   10

Chapter 3   14

Chapter 4   23

Chapter 5   28

Chapter 6   37

Chapter 7   45

Chapter 8   56

Chapter 9   62

Chapter 10   73

Chapter 11   83

Chapter 12   92

Chapter 13   99

Chapter 14   105

Chapter 15   113

Chapter 16	121
Chapter 17	128
Chapter 18	140
Chapter 19	150
Chapter 20	159
Chapter 21	164
Chapter 22	174
Chapter 23	184
Chapter 24	192
Chapter 25	198
Chapter 26	204
Chapter 27	212
Chapter 28	220
Chapter 29	228
Chapter 30	237
Chapter 31	243

About the Author

Being a sculptor has always been my creative outlet, even though my quiet moments have always been spent reading. As my aging hands and fingers found it difficult to manipulate clay and wood to the same degree, I knew I would need to find a new way to express my imaginative process.

Delving into memories and acknowledging that "I am not what has happened to me, but what I choose to allow to shape who I am," I saw the pendulum of my mind oscillate between sense and nonsense and embraced the journey.

Writing has become an outlet that has helped to nurture a new mode of creativity. Being creative is freeing in a way I don't think I will ever be able to explain, but it helps the soul to soar!

Chapter 1

Red silk swished past Bart at the front door of Club Coeur Noir, her hips brushing by the empty coat check counter and continuing on to the crowded bar. Gary, the bartender of the night smiled as he prepared her regular choice of Angel's Envy neat with a side glass of ice. Her auburn tresses draped over her bosom as she reached for the glass with a whisper, "Thanks honey."

Everyone knew of "Flame"! All eyes, male and female, followed her as she surveyed her prospects for the night. The "Red Room", her regular Thursday night reserved space, was just down the hall past the main observation area. One man in particular caught her eye. He stood at a towering 6 feet 3 inches, with wide, muscular shoulders and a chiseled physique. A fitted bespoke suit and polished black Italian loafers complemented his well-dressed appearance. His wavy, dark brown locks were mid-length with that one rebellious curl that fell over his forehead, with just the right amount of 5 o'clock shadow gracing his square jawline. The Adonis in the crowd turned and glanced over his shoulder with a smirk as the auburn-haired beauty motioned to him.

It was then she felt the warm breath of a silver fox on her ear. He whispered in a deep baritone, "You want a man, not a boy tonight, my love! Choose carefully." A chill ran down her spine as she turned and responded with, "Maybe another night, handsome. My choice has been made for tonight. Call me next week." as she slipped him her card. He looked down, seeing it was a card for "Calloway Art Gallery." He smiled and nodded his satisfaction.

Approaching the stranger at the end of the bar, she sashayed over with the perfect balance of allure with her red silk wrap dress revealing just the right amount of creamy decolletage and a peek of leg. As they stood face-to-face, their eyes locked in, the man smiled and extended his hand, saying, "You can call me Max." Skillfully evading his hand, she leaned in, whispering in his ear, "I'm known as Flame, and the Red Room will be ours in ten minutes." He nodded and asked if she would want another drink. Flashing his Black Amex card, he told Gary to put her drinks on his tab. *He looks like he may be fun for this Thursday's play date!* she thought, smiling, as she continued down the hall, stopping in front of the main observation window. Recognizing another set of regulars performing for the group of observers, she continued to her reserved Thursday night room.

She checked her watch and waited for Max to join her drinks in hand. Unlocking the door with her keycard, she adjusted the lighting to her liking. Then, using the remote by the door, she adjusted the music on the sound system to a soft and seductive level, playing her favorite blues sounds. As BB King crooned, "The Thrill Is Gone," she turned and asked Max if the song selection met with his approval. He nodded in agreement, not caring less about the background sounds. Loosening the tie at the waist of her dress, Flame opened the doors to the Toy closet. She looked over her shoulder with a coy smile and said, "We each have two choices of toys tonight." She removed the nipple clamps. "These little bad boys never fail to drive me wild," she explained to him. Then she removed the black silk Shibari rope from the wall. "I like a little tie-and-tease action, but nothing too violent. Just enough to spice things up, you know…"

Stepping back, she allowed Max time to peruse the wall of toys. Since she mentioned bondage, he chose the fur-lined handcuffs and then picked out the unfettered leather suspension harness with foot supports to be mounted from the ceiling apparatus. Flame smiled, agreeing with his choice. As he turned around to see her response, he was left wide-eyed by the black leather bustier she was wearing over the tiniest g-string. He knew she was built well but had no idea how lucky he was going to be to experience her tonight.

Flame gracefully swept her hair over her right shoulder, revealing the enticing curve of her left neck and her silk-like creme-colored skin. Her auburn tresses now just grazed her partially exposed right nipple, with the black leather accentuating her slender waist and ample bust. The exposed roundness of her buttocks was that of a Da Vinci angel with long legs ending in a pair of 4" stilettos.

If he wasn't careful, he would be drooling over his partner for this evening's pleasures.

She sauntered over to him as Max threw his jacket on the settee. Unbuttoning his shirt slowly, one button at a time, she removed his belt with one long pull. She acknowledged his warm smile with a smirk of her own and a wink. He waited for her to loosen his pants before dropping them to the floor and taking off his shoes. His socks disappeared as quickly as his boxers, displaying a thick erection. She purred, stating this match was worth the wait.

Remotely lowering the ceiling assembly to attach the harness, she deftly connected the two and climbed to test the apparatus, leaving the g-string on the floor where she had been standing. Max reached down, retrieved them and walked over to place them in his jacket pocket. When he returned to her, she instructed him to put his arms at his sides and relax as she began to gracefully tie his upper body with the silk rope. She explained the principle and art of Shibari, the Japanese art of knotting ropes on parts of the body. She fashioned a noose for his neck that only caused pressure when other parts of his body flexed. She continued down his torso, tying his arms across his chest and looping in his upper thighs, causing him to take a wide stance, which she explained he would need in order to balance.

Max was intrigued by her mastery of such an art but questioned, "How will I be able to touch you if my hands are restrained?"

"You won't. Trust the process. I promise you will enjoy it," she said, giggling.

Flame then went to the table for Max's drink and had him take a long sip, emptying the tumbler. Replacing it, she finished her bourbon as well. Smiling over her shoulder, she asked, "Shall we begin? I intend to take this very slowly." Max nodded, displaying faint dimples as he smirked at her. She then went to her hands and knees, crawling between his legs as she rubbed her silky tresses against his inner thighs, eliciting a moan. Buckling the harness around her waist and attaching the nipple clamps, she placed her feet in the stirrups of the harness and remotely lowered it to the correct height. She leaned over to kiss Max under his jaw on alternate sides and began licking certain areas of his chest before then lightly biting his nipples. Working her way down his body, bypassing strategic areas, the sultry redhead had Max growling and panting in no time. Raising the harness again remotely, Max was impressed with her practiced flexibility.

Flame then told Max to take the tie to her bustier into his mouth and pull. And as he did, it fell away from her body, affording him the first look at her exquisite nude form.

Max was already feeling ready to explode after the slow torture of her hands all over his body, as she worked the harness into different sensual configurations, licking and blowing air onto those areas while smiling up at him mischievously. Flame then lowered herself onto Max as she released her feet from the stirrups and wrapped her legs around his waist. She crossed her ankles behind his buttocks, pulling him tight to her core, and said, "Stand very still, and you will be rewarded." She strategically untied specific knots of the silk rope very slowly, tugging ever so slightly on the noose around his neck, literally taking his breath away briefly. Staring up at him with those luminous emerald orbs under long dark lashes, she ran her fingers through his dark locks and pulled him into a deep kiss. One more pull on the ropes, and they fell from his body. Unbuckling the harness, she whispered, "Now carry me to the red velvet bed, and I'm yours to do with as you please."

Max carried Flame like she weighed nothing. In four long strides, she was now on her back on the bed, exposed and aroused. Grabbing her hands to handcuff her to the pole at the bed's topside, Max placed her arms over her head, spread her hair across the pillow and reached over to the body oil on the adjacent table. Massaging the flavored oil onto her erogenous areas and kissing down her body, he found the turnabout was not only fair play but very exciting. "See how restraint can be intensely erotic?" Flame said to him with a teasing smile. Flipping her over, Max brought her ass into the air as he kissed down her spine and then licked behind her knees. He proceeded to put the tip in several times, making Flame aroused more than she ever thought was possible, before finally plunging into her. They both moaned and writhed in absolute pleasure as they found their release. Holding her tight to his body, he released her hands from the cuffs, and they fell to the bed, panting.

After catching their breath, in one languorous move, Flame slid from the bed. Max watched her hips sway as she sauntered to the phone on the wall and ordered a bottle of Louis Roederer Champagne and some dark chocolate truffles. Slipping her arms into the silk robe at the foot of the bed, she wrapped herself up and waited for the knock at the door. Taking the tray from a young man she didn't recognize, she carried it over to the bed, pouring two flutes. Flame then drank heartily as she smashed a truffle onto Max's ripped abdomen and proceeded to eat it off. He laughed, stating, "You are just full of surprises!" She met his eyes and smiled mischievously and gave him his flute that he took a sip from as she poured herself another.

They played back and forth with inventive ways to eat the chocolates. Using melted chocolate, he wrote his name across her thigh, later erasing it by licking it off with his tongue. She laughed and poured a third flute of champagne. Elevating herself onto her elbows, instead of lying flat on her back, she watched Max write on her body and then lick the chocolate off. He demonstrated inventive ways to play with her body, and she enjoyed it immensely. She would have to have a return trip with Max to the Red Room, named for its crimson velvet coverlet draped over satin sheets on the bed and complemented by the rich, deep red plush carpeting.

By 2:00 a.m., Flame was feeling very warm and sleepy. Her vision was blurring around the edges, and sounds were muffled. Claiming exhaustion, she began to put the toys away, cluing Max into the termination of their night. Max dressed and kissed her sweetly and passionately as he pulled her softness against his firm body. Grabbing his jacket and flinging it over his shoulder, he exited the room, stopping at the bar to pay for their evening's libations even though he didn't drink the champagne other than one sip.

Flame collapsed to the floor after locking the door, still naked. She heard male voices in the room, but that couldn't be. She thought she remembered locking the door before she fell into oblivion.

Chapter 2

What is that incessant pounding? My head hurts and is fuzzy enough without that pounding!

Attempting to open her eyes, Marissa (a.k.a. Flame) feels totally disoriented. *Is the pounding someone at the door, or is it the rhythmic pounding of machinery?* she wonders. Shaking herself awake, Marissa sneezes with the dust and odor of mold invading her senses. She is lying on a filthy mattress wrapped in a threadbare blanket in what appears to be a basement. *Where the hell am I, and how did I get here?*

Looking up at the single bare bulb on the ceiling, the only source of illumination, Marissa coughs again from the dust collected in her throat. Glancing around, she sees a small bottled water in front of the makeshift bed, which she opens and guzzles until dry. The thought then strikes her that the water may have been laced with something. Trying to gather her wits, she takes stock of her surroundings. Pulling her knees to her chest, she sighs in relief to find every body part moving and feeling normal. She realizes that she is dressed in only her wrap dress with no undergarments, and a shiver runs down her spine. *Who could have put me here?* she wonders in fear. Then she notices the large bucket at the end of the mattress and something wrapped in deli paper. When she unwraps the parcel, she finds a turkey club sandwich with extra bacon, lettuce and tomato on whole wheat bread; just the way she would order it. She feels frightened, realizing her captor must be someone who knows her well or has been following and watching her. Devouring the sandwich, Marissa looks at her wrist for her watch. Not only is her watch gone, but her ruby and diamond ring and diamond stud earrings are missing.

Marissa rises from the mattress to search for a door and makes her way to the wall farthest from the light source. With her arms outstretched, she feels her way down the wall until she comes to a large tub of some kind mounted on the wall. Using her hands to investigate, since it is pitch black beyond the mattress area, Marissa realizes it is a large laundry sink. She turns the faucet and out comes only cold water with little pressure. Nothing comes out of the hot side, *But hey, at least there is a water source,* she looks at the bright side.

Continuing around the perimeter, Marissa finds just an open expanse. There are no windows or doors that she can find. *How on earth did I even enter this place?* And, without windows, she has no way of knowing even the time of day. *Wait, how long was I unconscious? Is today Friday or another day?* The darkness envelops her until she is just yards from the mattress again.

After shaking some of the dirt from the blanket, Marissa wraps herself in it to trap some of her body heat. Screwing up her face in response to the mephitic odors in her confines she plants herself on the musty old mattress. She then takes stock of what she can remember. She dressed in her favorite red silk wrap dress and left home around 9:15. The sedan picked her up out front and took her to "Coeur Noir Club" for her regular Thursday night reservation of 10:00 p.m. in the "Red Room". She greeted Bart at the door, making her way past the empty cloakroom to saunter into the bar area. Gary had her regular "Angel's Envy" poured and waiting with her side of ice. She perused the room to find her playdate and landed on Max. They enjoyed hours in that room together.

"At least I can recall my night with Max if I feel down," Marissa mused.

Preparing to find her way around the room's perimeter again to count the approximate steps, she is hit with a wave of nausea and a feeling of succumbing to sleep again. She chastises herself for being complacent and just guzzling the water and eating without concern. *I've been drugged again* were the last thoughts she had before falling back on the mattress and succumbing to the blackness that enveloped her.

Waking sometime later, Marissa finds a bucket of what once probably was warm water, a washcloth and a towel. Lifting the towel, she notices some soap, a toothbrush and toothpaste. On the other side of the mattress is a small cooler filled with bottled water and fruit.

Alongside the cooler is another sandwich of corned beef and cheese on rye. She muses to herself, "A salad would have been nice". Laughing out loud, she thinks, *I've become a pretty demanding captive! I should be thankful they are giving me anything.*

This time, before drinking, Marissa holds each water bottle to the light, looking for punctures from a hypodermic.

Chapter 3

Cruising home, Roger glanced over at the cute little blonde in his Bentley with him. Reaching over, he ran his hand up her left leg as he grazed the apex of her thighs with his pinky finger. Tess pulled her skirt to her hips, putting her feet on the dashboard, revealing what Roger was searching for, exposed in the passing overhead street lights. "Let's make this easier, old man," she purred. "But keep your eyes on the road, and don't crash!" Taking his hand in hers and guiding it under her thong to the dampness between her thighs, she said: "This is yours later. Just remember you have a houseful of guests to entertain first when we get there." Reaching over, Tess softly stroked up Roger's thigh to his crotch as he groaned.

Pulling into the garage, Roger turned and said, "We can always just blow off this party." Tess laughed, staring down at Roger's tented slacks and said, "But it is here at your house. Do I need to make an adjustment for you before we go in?" Smiling, Roger opened the driver's side door. At the same time, Tess extracted herself from the passenger side, wiggling her dress back down her thighs and adjusting the neckline of her mini dress to expose more cleavage. With his palm on her ass, she smiled and went in through the garage door directly into the kitchen.

Max, Roger's best friend and attorney, scowled at Roger for bringing another "cupcake" to a social function. Tess, a 24-year-old Theresa Brown, was an obvious gold digger. Roger Macnamara was the 41-year-old owner and CEO of Mac Technologies, with a 1.25 billion dollar plus personal net worth. Roger introduced Tess around the room with a shrug in Max's direction. Max intoned, "We will speak privately later."

Standing at the kitchen counter, pouring himself another Macallan Scotch, Max overheard a conversation about the abduction of the renowned "Flame", the gorgeous redhead from an alternative lifestyle club two nights ago. Turning in the direction of the conversation, Max immediately recognized the silver-haired gentleman who had approached "Flame" just before they ventured back to the Red Room. In turn, the gentleman recognized Max, grabbing his arm and directing him to the vacant library. Pulling his arm free, Max demanded to know what this is was about. The "Silver Fox" introduced himself as Mark Winslow, a private investigator hired by Cyrus and Felix Newcomb, owners of Coeur Noir Club.

Describing the events after Max left the club, Mark wanted to know how Max knew "Flame". Max recounted the story of having just joined the club and experiencing his first night there as one he will never forget. That redhead had taken up residence in his mind on an erotic loop. Mark smiled and said she was the most desired woman at the club but was very selective in who she would "play" with. Mark lamented never having had an evening with her yet. Max asked if there was anything he could do to help the investigation since he did have access to legal sources that Mark may not have immediate access to. Exchanging cards, they agreed to meet here to talk tomorrow morning.

As the evening wound down, Max climbed into his restored custom silver Mercedes 450 coupe and made his way back to his penthouse. He stood staring out the floor-to-ceiling glass window in his bedroom, playing his evening with Flame over again in his mind on a loop. Just thinking of her again aroused him. His concern for her after hearing she had been abducted caused a knot in his stomach. He needed to do something to help find her and knew he would have a sleepless night thinking about what he could contribute to help locate her. He then vowed to call both Roger and Mark and have them convene at Roger's townhouse in order to paint a full picture of what needs to be done.

While back at Roger's brownstone, Roger and Tess fell into bed at almost dawn after too much drinking and socializing. Come morning, Roger stirred without disturbing Tess when his phone buzzed on his nightstand. Seeing it was Max, he went to the en suite to call him back.

Tess woke to the sounds of water running in the en suite shower. Rising and wiping the melted mascara from under her eyes, she sauntered in, opening the glass door to the shower, surprising Roger. She stepped in front of him and dropped to her knees with a smirk and her palms on his thighs. He lifted her to her feet, stating he was running late, and stepped out of the shower, telling her to take her time. Hanging a soft terry cloth robe and towel on the hook just outside of the shower door, he went to the bedroom to dress. Tess washed away the party effects from last night and could smell coffee brewing when she exited the shower. Wrapping the oversized robe around her, she walked downstairs to the kitchen. Swishing through the door, letting the robe swing open, she stood dazed with dripping wet hair, staring down at a mug and note. The note was to the point. ***"Had fun, ordered you a sedan, will call later. Take the money for your breakfast. R"*** Lifting the note, a hundred-dollar bill fluttered to the floor. Turning in an arch to see if Roger was anywhere around, Tess cursed, took the money and stomped upstairs to quickly dress. Taking the stairs in quick succession, she called him several names loudly as she exited through the front door after hearing the sedan honking outside. Tess slammed the door as a final statement, missing Roger's chuckle in the home office.

He stood there with Max, waiting for Mark's arrival. Max asked if Roger had eaten and made his way to the kitchen. Rattling a few pans as he worked, Max put together a basic bacon and eggs with toast. He carried both plates to the dining table, calling Roger. Halfway through the meal, the front doorbell sounded. Roger jumped up, looking out of the sidelight windows to see Mark standing with a cardboard carrier of three coffee cups from the "Witches Brew" coffee house just outside of Georgetown.

As the three men settled in again at the table, Max grabbed his briefcase with his folio to record any pertinent information. Mark started off with, "Let me enlighten you both on the details. Flame is actually Marissa Calloway of the Calloway Art Gallery in Georgetown. Her home is located just two blocks from the gallery at 3139 N St. N.W. She is an heiress, and that may be the impetus of the abduction, but nothing is certain."

Roger smirked at the sarcastic tone of Mark's voice. Max just bristled! Max inquired about the overall knowledge of what had happened and who had started to look into it. "So far, the doorman/bouncer Bart has been questioned," Mark said, "the Thursday night bartender Gary has been called in to give his story, and of course, the club owners Felix and Cyrus Newcomb are the ones who have contacted me to request a discreet investigation. The security camera feeds have been turned over to me, but I am yet to watch them." Roger then suggested they go into his home office, where he has state-of-the-art equipment to use.

Setting up the feed, Roger commented that someone had finally spent enough money on the security cameras to have a decent resolution. The three watched Flame and Max walk down the hallway to enter the Red Room. Roger, of course, commented to Max, "What the hell did you do to deserve that hot little momma?" Max just smiled and said, "Right?" Mark cleared his throat and explained that Flame is the most desired female member of the club, but very discerning. Her pickiness irritates a good many men and even women who would like to spend an evening with her.

Max then commented, "That is how we initially met." Roger looked at them quizzically, causing both Max and Mark to laugh. Max then asked Mark, "What was it that you said to her when I went to get her drink?" Mark replied, "Choose carefully sweetheart. You want a man, not a boy." To which Max's retort was, "And that is exactly what she did." Mark then commented, "Touche!" causing all three of them to chuckle in unison. Max then paused, looking up at Mark, saying, "How is it you were there that night?" Mark then pulled out his wallet showing Max his club membership card dating back three years. "That is how long I have been waiting for a chance with that vixen in the Red Room on her regular Thursday night," said Mark.

After the feed started back up, a young man, obviously aware of the cameras, was seen hiding his face as he served the champagne and truffles. There was then a reasonable lull in activity. The next action was Max leaving the room with his jacket slung over his shoulder, wearing a smile. He stopped at the bar to settle his bill and then left, slapping a hefty tip on the bar for Gary. The time stamp was 2:37 a.m. There was no more activity until two men appeared, hiding their faces from the camera and unlocking the door using a keycard at 3:48 a.m. They reappeared carrying a limp redhead wrapped loosely in the dress she had been wearing earlier, and carry her from the club to a waiting black sedan with no plates visible. "We think we found the man wearing the gray herringbone coat walking towards the club earlier on a traffic cam. They need to run facial recognition on him a.s.a.p.," said Roger, thinking out loud.

At this point, Max was pacing back and forth in his "Legal sleuth mode". Mark then explained that one major concern was finding blood all over the Red Room. He said there would be a forensics team in there today to go over the room. Max sat down heavily on the nearest chair, hearing about blood being found. Looking up at Mark, Max asks, "Shouldn't we get to the club to see what Forensics comes up with?" Agreeing that would be a good next move, they all pile into Roger's Bentley. Max gave him directions and kept firing questions at Mark. "Whoa counselor," Mark responded, "you are getting ahead of yourself!" Shaking his head, Max stated that he was not trying to be forward.

Pulling out his phone and checking emails that he hadn't paid attention to all weekend, Max turned to Mark, showing him the screen. "What the hell does this mean?" The email was cryptic, stating, ***"She must pay, and you know how!"*** Max then explained that that particular email was to a joint business account that he and Roger shared. *Who would have sent that on Friday night? Was this related to "Flame"/Marissa's disappearance?* Max wondered. Roger then told Max to forward that to the Mac Tech weekend team to have them trace the origin and call Jason there to update him. "Tell him it is a priority, put as many on it as needed!"

Parking directly in front of the club, the three exited the car and entered the club without anyone detaining them. Cyrus and Felix were propped up at the bar. Each with a coffee in hand discussing how to handle this whole debacle. Seeing Mark, they started over, motioning for everyone to sit at a table, ordering coffee for everyone and asking Gary, the Thursday night bartender, to join them. They then started from the beginning. Gary admitted that he had no idea who the young man was that delivered the champagne to the Red Room. He admitted that he put the bottle and glasses on a tray and got busy with patrons. When he noticed the tray was gone, he figured the kitchen person delivered it along with the truffles.

While sitting there, the forensics team finished up, and the lead stopped at the table. After a quick in-room test, it appeared that the blood found was not human. Primary testing showed it as pig's blood. The champagne bottle contents were laced with a heavy amount of Phenobarbital. Everything was to be sent to the lab for priority 1 testing, and they would know the results definitively by later today.

As the forensics team departed, all eyes went to Max. "How is it you were not affected by the Phenobarbital, Max?" were the first words Felix muttered since they sat down. Max smiled and said "I simply don't care for champagne, and only had the smallest sip not to appear ungrateful!" Roger interjected, "I can attest to that. I have known Max since he was 12. He never drinks champagne."

Chapter 4

Enjoying the tepid water to wash with, Marissa is still picking blood from under her fingernails. *I can't recall any blood being shed. How is it that my dress is stained and my hands are covered with blood? And whose blood is it?* Feeling overcome by the whole scenario, Marissa brings her knees to her chest, drops her face into her hands on her knees and begins to sob. "How could this have happened to me? Where am I, and who would have done this?" The overwhelming depressive feelings have taken her to a very dark place reminiscent of her early childhood. But those emotions and memories have been buried for so long, how is it they are surfacing now?

Marissa can feel the belt again as it strikes her buttocks and thighs. She is cowering from the attack! She can just barely remember being locked in the wine cellar for hours without light, listening to the tiny beasts scurrying past her feet. The fear is just overpowering as she finds herself drawn into a tight knot of arms and legs, hearing her father demean her again and again from the doorway! "I'm sorry Pappa! I will be your angel from now on! Please Pappa, I love you!" That voice of a tiny girl crying out is still in the back of her mind. She tells herself, "I am not that girl anymore. I am a self-sufficient, successful woman! Pack those memories back in the dark recesses and move on!"

With her resolve bolstered again, Marissa wipes the tears from her face with the back of her hand and rises. She takes off her blood-stained dress, wrapped in a blanket and makes her way hand over hand to the laundry sink in the depths of her prison to launder it and hang it to dry over the sink side.

The lack of daylight is disconcerting and makes her feel like Alice in Wonderland at times. The intermittent drugging doesn't help this situation. As long as she doesn't start seeing the glowing eyes of the "Cheshire cat," she will persevere.

Smiling to herself, she tries to put together some kind of plan. She will first count the steps it takes her to traverse the perimeter of her confines. Next she will clean her little corner of the world so she is not always suffering from the mold and dust in her nose. *If only it was just possible for me to reach the ceiling to see if there are any other light bulbs that are not turned on. Maybe while counting my steps, I can find a light switch or electrical panel.*

Having a resourceful mind, Marissa uses the end of her toothbrush to scribe the number of steps into the dust by the wall across from her bed. Avoiding stepping on her work, she makes her way around again, feeling for a switch where the darkness prevails. This endeavor takes quite some time since she has to feel up, down and over each surface. Her hands feel like sandpaper doing this, and she has abraded several fingers to the extent of them seeping blood at the tips. Intermittently, sticking one in her mouth to suck on it, she keeps going. Midway across the rear wall, just past the sink, she finds a switch that doesn't appear to work anything. But, at least she knows there is possibly another source of illumination in the back of her cinder block prison. As if this is going to benefit her without access to another light bulb and the ability to reach the ceiling. Just when she is feeling positive about her findings, reality sets back in. Although, this information may prove to be important if she is confined down here for a very long time. *Now THAT'S a thought that can elicit depression!*

Having made her way around the room fully, Marissa plops onto her mattress, causing a cloud of dust to mushroom into the air. Coughing, she decides to attempt to beat the dust out of the mattress. Marissa then drags the mattress over to the side wall. Using the small towel to cover her mouth and nose, she attempts to lift the mattress and turn it to lean against the side wall. This whole process was much easier to accomplish in her mind than in reality. But Marissa was determined, if nothing else! After several attempts at upending the mattress, she accepted the alternative. Dropping it on the floor several times did appear to dislodge quite a bit of the dust. At this point, her entire nude body was covered with dirt from her efforts, so she ventured to the back with the soap and washcloth to use the cold water from the laundry to clean up. "Certainly not a luxury spa," were her words to no one but herself "But, beggars can't be choosers. I'll take cold water over none any day!" And with that admission, she mused, "And, now I'm talking to myself out loud! Just amazing!"

Hearing footfalls above her head, she rushed to pull her still-damp dress on and hurry back to the mattress. Getting there just in time to see a ceiling hatch open, she mused, "So that's how I got down here!" A ladder was lowered, and several pairs of legs were visible at the opening. Marissa was trying to think about what she could use as a weapon if needed. Her stilettos would have been perfect if only she had them here. Then, stunned, she watched the familiar bald head descend. Jonathan Abrams, her gallery manager, turned with a smirk, causing her to growl at him. "What the hell, Jonathan? Why would you do this? Do you really think you will get away with this?"

He never even responded with words, he just stuck a hypodermic into her neck. As the blackness took her over, Marissa fell back only to be caught in his arms and laid back on the mattress.

Jonathan then spoke under his breath, "Don't want to hurt you, my dear. I just need you as leverage." Then Jonathan told the men at the top of the ladder to hand down the supplies. He covered Marissa with a fresh blanket and changed out the bucket she had been using as a toilet with a fresh portable potty bucket with a seat, some biodegradable toilet paper, another cooler with water and even juice this time, a single-serve salad, and lastly a clean pair of sweatpants and top. *Hopefully this would suffice until someone from his team could get back here again,* he thought to himself.

Waking later, Marissa wallowed in self-pity. "How is it everytime I trust someone explicitly, they betray me in such a grand fashion? I don't even know why! Who else from the gallery is involved?"

Chapter 5

Driving home from the club was silent! No one could understand what they had learned. Agreeing to meet later for dinner would afford them each time to put their thoughts and questions together.

Roger offered the services of his tech team and resources, knowing he had the best team available, even better than the government. After all, he had a contract with the DEA, DOD and DOJ, supplying them with the most updated software and training. His people were the best of the best, and he would gladly pay the overtime for their expertise!

Max offered his connections to Mark. He could get a search warrant through his friends, who were judges, at any time of the night or day. He also had the ability to obtain any legal background information at any time needed. Figuring the most important thing he offered was his legal mind and ability to read people after so many years of litigation, depositions and interrogatories.

It was decided that the three men would meet at Fiorino's for some Italian fare. Max knew the owner, or rather, was distantly related to Sergio, so he requested the intimate back room. Arriving fifteen minutes early, Max sauntered into the kitchen, interrupting Sergio's tirade at the cook. Smiling at him, Sergio warmly hugged Max, saying it had been too long since they connected. They both promised to catch up within the next week. Max left the kitchen and headed to the bar. Sergio followed him and told him to go enjoy the back room. It will be theirs exclusively tonight, and there was already a selection of reds and glasses waiting. Perusing the wine choices on the side table, Max chose a Sangiovese Chianti and poured a hefty amount into his wine glass. Drinking deeply, he was attempting to quell his anxiety over the missing woman haunting his thoughts.

Roger was next to arrive, shown to the back room by the hostess. Max wasn't sure, but it looked like Roger got her number on the way in. Smiling at Roger, Max declared, "What is with you and picking up the cupcakes?" Roger laughed and stated, "You never know when one might be the next Mrs. Macnamara." Max just shook his head as Mark was shown into the room.

They all enjoyed a great meal in spite of the stressful information being exchanged. After the second bottle of wine was consumed, Mark disclosed that the one man caught on camera had been identified as Jonathan Abrams, who was actually the gallery manager for Marissa over the past three years. That stung, being a betrayal within the work family. The three men agreed that Mark would go to the gallery tomorrow morning and interview the staff. He reported that he had been there Saturday morning and was told by none other than

Abrams that the boss (Marissa) was on vacation in Greece. When going in tomorrow morning, Mark will interview only Janet Mayfield, the back-office worker and gallery setup coordinator. Skipping dessert, they all departed, promising to reconnect by phone at the end of tomorrow.

On the way out the door, Sergio called out to Max, alerting him to the fact that someone had just come in twenty minutes prior, asking if Max was there after seeing his car in the lot. Max asked for his description, and Sergio claimed he could do one better. "Come into my office and view the closed-circuit video." It was obvious to Max who it was by the defining bald head! Jonathan Abrams was looking for him. *But why?* Before leaving he called Mark to alert him to this fact. And with trepidation, Max walked to his car, checking the undercarriage and all around the vehicle before getting in. Paranoia was becoming a regular part of his world now.

In spite of the hour, Mark and Roger met Max at his condo to discuss this new wrinkle. Roger let himself into the elevator using his keycard, then remembered Mark wouldn't be able to do the same. Stepping back out of the elevator, Roger waited for Mark to arrive. Mark, being impressed already by the 601 Wharf St. S.W. address, stepped off of the private elevator right into Max's double penthouse suite. Impressed with the floor-to-ceiling windows affording a spectacular view of the city lights reflected on the Potomac, Mark walked closer to see the few sloops still out on the water in full sail and vibrant spinnaker, sailing across the moon-streaked waters. Taken by the view, he turned to speak to Roger, losing all memory of what he was ready to say. The expanse of the open floor plan of a 4,400-square-foot penthouse was awe-inspiring! The kitchen gleamed with stainless steel and black marble countertops. The floors, as far as Mark could see, were black, gray and white swirled marble with gorgeous Aubusson rugs to delineate the areas. The live edge olive wood table with a Chihuly glass fixture over it glistened in the light. The deep burgundy leather sofa and gray leather barrel chairs surrounded a glass and chrome 48" square cocktail table. The wall behind the chairs sported a very large Warhol painting. Going up close, Mark saw the undeniable signature. He didn't openly articulate his thoughts: "So, this is how the top 5% live?"

Turning to see Max walking down the hall, Roger and Mark were beckoned into the home office. The decor in there was much more of what Mark would have expected. The back wall was an expanse of mahogany bookcases exhibiting a variety of legal resource books as well as a few shelves of beautifully bound leather first-edition novels. Stepping closer, Mark pointed to a framed photo of two young men deepwater fishing, each holding a large fish. Mark asked, "You and Roger?" Max smiled and said, "We have been best friends for the past 25 years. So, yes, my brother!" The next photo was of them hang-gliding at age 20 something. Max then directed Mark to the deep chocolate brown leather Chesterfield sofa in front of the carved antique mahogany desk. The channel-backed office chair spun to accommodate Max as he sat. Remotely lighting the Tiffany lamps strategically placed around the room, he asked if anyone wanted anything from the bar as Roger opened a carved wooden cabinet to display a collection of crystal decanters. Mark said he wouldn't object to a brandy. Max told Roger he would join in on that. Passing the snifters out, Roger sat on the opposing end of the Chesterfield sofa.

Max addressed the paranoia he was feeling after hearing that Jonathan Abrams asked for him at Fiorino's earlier that evening. That indicated to him that he was being watched and followed for whatever reason. Just then, Max's and Roger's phones indicated a joint email again. Facing the others as the color drained from his face, Max declared another cryptic message was coming in. This time, it was two lines: ***"You are the only source of hope for our little miss! Hope you are up to it!"***

Roger immediately shot the message over to MAC Tech and called Jason again. Max and Mark cringed when Roger declared double week's pay for whoever cracks this first at headquarters! Smiling, Roger said, "We should hear something momentarily. Money motivates."

Mark decided they needed to lighten the mood. He asked about Max and Roger's background and how they met. Roger laughed and said, "Max was the only child of the wealthiest family in Milan. He was shipped off to boarding school when he was 12 because of threats of abduction in Milan. Born Maximillian Giovani Corleone, he was tutored within the family compound until that time. Max spoke English, Italian, French, German and Greek fluently and could interpret Latin by the time he started school here in the States. At twelve, he was placed in my class, three grades ahead of the others his age. Of course, feeling alone and isolated, I took him under my wing."

Max then laughed and said, "The devil's spawn welcomed me into his lair!" He continued to narrate that they were inseparable after that first year together. They graduated together and went on to room together at Harvard undergrad. "Roger then went on to business and computer science, and I went into law and graduated from Harvard Law." Roger then interjected, "Top of his class in both undergrad and grad school and valedictorian." Max then reciprocated with, "And Roger started his own technologies company before he even graduated from the program!" Mark laughed, saying "Duly impressed by both, and glad to have you on my team to help with this."

Max excused himself to take a call. So, Roger and Mark continued the tour of the penthouse. Turning down the hall toward the primary bedroom suite, Roger threw open the carved double doors. The room was a soft gray with charcoal plush carpeting underfoot that you literally sank into. The carved oversized four-poster king bed stood freely in the center of the room. It was surrounded by walls of art and another massive Chihuly glass fixture overhead displaying layers of massive glass leaves in blues and grays. There were two small smoked glass cylindrical tables on either side of the head of the bed, just large enough for a glass of wine and the phone stand and remote controller that graced each. There was a royal blue velvet bench at the foot of the bed, the same color as the royal blue velvet bed comforter that dipped to the floor, concealing the drawers at the base of the bed. The far wall opposite the bed afforded the same spectacular floor-to-ceiling glass view of the Potomac with heavy striped gray, white and royal blue velvet light-blocking drapes that adjusted remotely.

Using the switch by the closet door, Roger illuminated the two smoked glass tables by the bed for an ambient light source. Opening the closet doors, Roger announced, "This is the piece de resistance," lighting the central glass bureau, illuminated from within. Each drawer held color-coordinated shirts with ties and silk pocket squares. Each section also had drawers under those with color-coordinated underwear and socks. On top was another glass case showing a splendid watch collection. The hanging clothing sections around the three closet walls were all behind glass doors. Roger informed that each was climate-controlled, with coordinating shoes beneath each colored collection of suits or casual wear.

As if not impressed enough, Mark, alngside Roger, entered a state-of-the-art exercise room before turning into the largest ensuite bathroom he had ever seen. The shower alone was the size of a small bedroom with swirled marble walls made of the same imported marble on the floors in the other rooms. All of the floors were radiantly heated, and the shower had a dozen shower heads that Mark could count. Across from the shower was a 10-foot-long counter with smoked glass vessel sinks and waterfall spigots that were operated by motion sensors. Going through another smoked glass door led to a room for just a toilet and bidet. When you closed the door, the glass became opaque. Adjacent to that was a huge walk-in bath that could accommodate at least four average-sized people, also completed in marble with a river-rock waterfall at the far end to fill the tub with water heated by the solar collection units on the roof.

The entire expanse of the exterior facing the Potomac was a ten-foot-deep balcony the length of the main area and bedroom. This was all undercover to afford a weather-free place to sit and enjoy the view. Once I picked my jaw up from the floor, I turned to Roger and questioned, "Just how rich was the richest family in Milan?" He laughed and said at least six generations of compounded wealth over the years. Max has never needed to work, but won't stop for any reason! When his parents died, he sold everything within and all properties and compounds owned in Europe, which were nine that I knew of. He invested everything here in the states, which he said was the only home he wanted. He likes his luxury, but never goes overboard by his standards. He likes to travel, but is reserved even with that. I on the other hand would be over the top if I had his resources. And, mine aren't too shabby!

With that narrative, I told Roger we would meet up tomorrow when it was convenient for them. "Just point me in the direction I need to go. I'll see you with fresh eyes tomorrow." He said to meet at his brownstone tomorrow for breakfast. Say around 10? I nodded and waved goodnight as the elevator doors closed.

Chapter 6

Max

Driving to Roger's at 9:30 in the morning would have been fine had my mind been where it should have been. Not sleeping well while thinking constantly about Marissa didn't help my concentration. All I could think of was how good she felt in my arms and how we were so in sync together both physically as well as mentally and emotionally. I was paying no attention to the dark van that had been flanking me the entire drive. Pulling up to Roger's house, I even forgot to grab my phone out of the car holder. Remembering at the last second, I turned back to my car, reaching into the interior when the van screeched to a stop beside me, throwing open the side door. Before I even had time to react, there was a pinch in my neck from a hypodermic, and my world went immediately black. Thrown into the van, I was evidently trussed up and gagged on the floor as the van pulled out of the Sheridan Kalorama Historic District.

Roger must have just thrown open the door when he saw me pull up. He caught the whole scene in vivid technicolor and dramatic slow motion in spite of the van peeling wheels leaving his street. The only thing he could remember were the last three digits of a Virginia tag *637*. He was on the phone with the police and Mark immediately. And the decision was made to bring in the FBI. An heiress and a prominent D.C. attorney being abducted in one week made even Cyrus and Felix agree that this could no longer be kept under wraps! Roger's next call was to Mac Technologies to have them pull all traffic cams up in the area to try and track down that van.

The emails that had been coming in were tracked to the public library's IP address. Of course, a fake name and driver's license were used as identification for the use of public computers. We needed to get a break here soon with the cameras and tracing the emails, or we were going to be chasing ghosts. All of this technology would be useless if we didn't soon find something traceable!

Before Roger could complain too much, Mark was running up his front steps. Directly behind him were several black SUVs with blue jackets emblazoned with acronyms jumping out of them, flooding the street. They were reminiscent of ants at a picnic, rushing single file from their vehicles. Right behind them was a police cruiser with two officers sent to take the report about the abduction. Watching from the front window, the officers were not happy with the FBI dismissing them so quickly. There was some back and forth by radio before the officers relented and drove away, leaving the blue jackets swarming over Max's car and terrorizing the neighborhood busybodies.

As the FBI lead on this case entered the front door of Roger's brownstone, we could hear others yelling instructions up the street and directing neighbors to go inside their homes until they were approached by an agent. Lionel Sharpe, The FBI lead introduced himself and asked us to sit down and give him the play-by-play. We graciously took our seats and proceeded to tag team, filling in the information.

Mark gave the moment by moment recount of that infamous Thursday night at the alternative lifestyle club Coeur Noir to raised eyebrows. While recounting the story with the video we had reviewed, Lionel had a grave expression on his face. He then peppered us with questions about Max and his background, drawing some ire from his best friend, Roger. I tried to soften the questioning by giving Lionel as much history of Max as I saw pertinent. Roger, I could see, was not pleased with the cynicism being shown by Lionel. I asked Roger if he would let me walk with Lionel to Max's car while he made some coffee. He relented, and that afforded me time to put Lionel in his place.

Once outside, I told Lionel that I believed he had walked into a situation with preconceived ideas and needed to loosen up and open his mind. He took a deep breath and nodded his ascent. I proceeded to describe Max and Roger's relationship and give Lionel the background he would need on Max. Describing his family background and the amount of wealth that he grew up with started

Lionel's mind in a new direction. Explaining the complexity of the case, with Marissa Calloway being the first one abducted from the club and then Max grabbed right in front of Roger's brownstone in the Sheridan Kalorama Historic district, put some perspective on the case. Lionel then asked how long Max and Roger had known each other. Describing their relationship did shed some light on Roger's reaction to Lionel's questioning.

Returning to Roger's front door, Lionel began over again with an apology for his terseness in the original fact-finding session. Roger then gave Lionel his card with his direct line handwritten on it. He explained that his company, Mac Technologies, designed the software used by most of the government agencies and he would be instrumental in any research needed. Lionel raised his eyebrow and smirked at Roger, causing Roger to explain that his people would be faster and more efficient, prioritizing this case. They would also be available at all times since they run shifts 24/7 without bureaucratic red tape. Lionel then understood and thanked Roger. Mark just smiled and handed Lionel his card, also stating he would hope to be kept in the loop at all times, particularly since he had to report back to the owners of Coeur Noir Club.

After sitting down again in the living room to discuss how this investigation would proceed, they were interrupted by a female agent who had gone over Max's car. She handed Lionel the cell phone that was still in the hands-free holder of the vehicle. Roger offered to unlock the phone using his biometrics since he and Max both used the same locking mechanism. Lionel again appeared perplexed, and Roger explained that for the last 25 years, he and Max were basically inseparable and shared all of their security with each other since they were each other's backup for everything. Roger then remembered to share the emails that they had received since this began last Thursday night. He explained that his team traced them to the central public library, where whoever sent them signed in with a fraudulent ID. The team was currently in the process of going through traffic cam footage to see if anyone could be identified in that area in the pertinent time frame.

Roger then remembered that Max's files for former cases were at his penthouse office. Asking if it would be useful for him to go through them to see if anything popped up, he suggested they all go there next. Mark smiled and asserted that Lionel would benefit from going with him and Roger. Lionel commandeered one of the SUVs, and they drove to Max's building. Entering the lobby, Roger directed Lionel to the last elevator. Using his keycard and thumbprint for entry, he turned to Mark and said that he would disarm the security as soon as the elevator stopped, requesting they wait until that was done to disembark. Lionel was startled by the extreme security measures and just looked at Mark, reading his expression. Mark just said, "You'll understand in a moment."

Mark observed Lionel's reaction as they were ushered into the Penthouse unit. Lionel just stood in awe as they entered the open-concept living, dining, and kitchen area. Immediately walking to the floor-to-ceiling windows where the Potomac was illuminated by the moonlight reflecting on the inky still water, Lionel asked, "Are we sure the primary abductee wasn't meant to be Mr. Corleone?" Roger and Mark both laughed, stating, "Practically no one understands the wealth behind Max. He lives very low-key unless you know him very well." Lionel then walked over to the large Warhol on the wall and asked, "Is this thing real?" To which Mark responded, "One of many."

Roger then redirected them to the home office. Once inside, he offered them a drink from the bar. Lionel mumbled something about still being on the clock. Roger then opened a panel in the bookcase that revealed an extensive filing system in chronological order of cases handled within the past 10 years. He then disclosed that years prior to that time frame were on microfilm in the safe. Mark then raised the question of where that would be. Roger then walked them back to the primary bedroom closet and, using biometrics again, unlocked one of the drawers below the last glass closet door. Lionel stood there watching and murmured under his breath, "Is he a James Bond enthusiast?" Roger just smiled, revealing that many of his clients are extremely wealthy and private, celebrities and dignitaries alike, whom Max takes incomparable care of.

Stepping out of the closet, Lionel scanned the room, questioning again about the art. Roger smiled, stating, "All originals! Most were from the family estates that Max inherited." Whistling, Lionel responded, "I thought this lifestyle was only in movies." Roger smirked, responding, "Max lives a very modest existence from what he came from. He hasn't got a pretentious bone in his body." Exiting the bedroom and walking down the hall towards the office again, Lionel noted the photos of Max with the Sheikh bin Sultan Al Nahyan of the United Arab Emirates, two different Presidents, several different movie and sports celebrities, and even saw Max with Pope Francis. Smiling, he just shook his head.

When back in the office, Roger handed each man a year of files to peruse, looking for something connecting this case to a former one. A half-hour in, Mark yelled, "Bingo!" Lifting the file, he said, "Max was called in as a consultant on a suit between the Calloway Gallery and this Shell company that Max identified as being owned by Malcolm Calloway the 3rd. That is Marissa's father isn't it?"

Roger said to keep digging; if there was one he was called in on, there were probably others. No more than ten minutes later, another case surfaced. The old man tried to block a very important acquisition by the Gallery using another Shell Corp that Max traced back to him. This was beginning to show promise!

Lionel looked up and said, "I'll take that drink now!" Mark laughed and stated the obvious: "Max probably didn't even connect Marissa to his previous cases since he knew her as "Flame" and not Marissa Calloway. He stepped into a hornet's nest without even being aware of it. Do you think her father would be behind her abduction and Max's?" Mark looked up and flushed with the realization that her father had been trying to undermine her all along, and Max helped to win her cases without realizing he was doing it! *Damn!*

"Just how far back do you think this has gone? And is Marissa even aware that her father has been trying to sabotage her?" Lionel asked

"Tomorrow morning, one of us needs to talk to Janet Mayfield at the gallery to see what she knows and how long she has worked there," Roger stated. Lionel looked up and said, "Let me take the lead on this. You two keep going through files. We need to know how extensively Max was involved."

Chapter 7

Again, there were footsteps overhead and what sounded like someone or something being dragged across the floor. Marissa was reluctant to just lie on the mattress and wait to be drugged, so she ran to the wall and followed it to the back, hiding in the shadows. Observing the hatch being opened and the ladder being lowered, she squinted, trying to take in the picture of her captor as he descended the ladder. *Was that the younger man who delivered the Champagne to the Red Room on that infamous night?* He stopped at the bottom, and someone's limp body was lowered down to him so he could intercept it before it fell, causing injury. Marissa recognized the body as Max. The younger man then dragged the body over to the mattress and tossed it on. A parcel was then lowered to the base of the ladder as the young man ascended again before the ladder was withdrawn.

Marissa then returned to the mattress to check on Max. He was still unconscious, dressed in jeans and a cashmere sweater; he still looked delicious! Her next quest was to find out what the parcel contained. She untied it carefully, finding two sandwiches and two sets of sweats, she sighed. One was smaller than the other, so Marissa pulled the shirt over her head and donned the pants, pulling the string inside to tighten them so they almost fit. Rolling the sleeves to expose her hands, she giggled and murmured, "At least they are warm...no fashion statement to be made!" With that, she heard Max grumble, "You look beautiful in anything."

"You're awake!" Max chuckled and mumbled, "With a massive headache!" Marissa responded, "I'm so sorry, but my pharmacy ran out of aspirin yesterday. But I can try to help you with acupressure."

Stepping over the rest of the parcel, Marissa approached Max, saying, "It is so good to see you again, but I figured we would meet the next time at the Club for a repeat of our evening." She handed Max a bottle of water and sat on the edge of the mattress. After guzzling ⅔ of the liquid, Max said, "Let me see if I remember correctly, your name is actually Marissa Calloway?" She nodded and asked how he knew. Max then launched into the story of what has happened since her abduction.

Marissa was pleased to know that she had been the focus of an investigation. When Max talked about the videos that have been gone through, Marissa stated that she didn't realize there were cameras in the club's public areas. She smirked when Max told her about the club owners hiring Mark Winslow, the man who tried to dissuade her from taking Max into the red room. He even described how he was cornered at Roger's party on Friday night, where Mark had been talking about the case to a gentleman at the kitchen island.

"I don't understand how you are down here?" Max then explained how he and Roger were working with Mark to try to find her. He added that he doesn't understand why he was grabbed. Maybe if they both gave some background information to each other, it would come to light.

Marissa then launched into her story between mouthfuls of her "cloak and dagger" sandwich, appropriately named for their circumstance. It was just a corned beef and Swiss on rye with coleslaw on it, but the other name suited it better! She recited a 30-year autobiography of Marissa Eleanor Calloway. She recanted her strong relationship with her mother, since her father was often away on business, growing up in New York City. Marissa described life in the Central Park South area and going to school at Marymount all girls school up until she graduated high school. She went on to Wellesley College in Massachusetts for undergraduate studies and on to Stanford for her master's in Art History. She explained how whenever she was off of school, they would travel to either the villa in Mykonos, Greece or the one in the Salamanca district of Madrid, Spain. She glowed when talking about her vacations with both parents in these locations. Tears then took the place of her smile as she talked about her mother's fatal battle with cancer during the end of Marissa's senior year at Stanford. Choking up and sobbing, she couldn't continue and melted into Max's shoulder for some comfort. Being embarrassed by her reaction, she wiped the tears away with the back of her hand and apologized for her emotional breakdown. She explained that she hadn't cried about that for years since dealing with it in Lanie's (her therapist) office. She explained how she was the sole beneficiary of her mother's insurance policy, and how she bought her townhouse in Georgetown and started her gallery with the funds. She smiled and said, "I was fortunate to have grown up sheltered and affluent in New York City."

Turning to Max, she said, "Your turn!" Max then explained that very few people are aware of his background, and he asked her not to repeat any of his history except the current one. He then began with his full name, Maximilian Giovani Corleone and the explanation that for at least 6 generations, his family was the wealthiest in Milan, Italy. As a child, he was sequestered to the family's compound for his safety (or so it was told). He was homeschooled and learned to speak English, French, Spanish, Greek and German fluently and to read Latin. He explained how, at the age of 12, he was shipped off to Woodberry Forest boarding school in Virginia. That was where he met and became brothers and best friends with Roger Macnamara. He described how he was placed several years beyond the norm in school and was taken under-wing by Roger. From there, Max went on to Harvard and then to Harvard Law. His parents were killed by a car bomb when he was a senior at Harvard, and he explained how he then sold their properties and almost all of their contents to remain here in the U.S.

Marissa questioned, "Properties, plural? How many did they have?" Max appeared to blush, stating, "Milan and Sorrento in Italy, Athens in Greece; Zurich and St. Cergue in Switzerland; Nice and Monaco in France; Munich in Germany; Sant Cugat del Vallès in Barcelona province, Spain; And lastly, Luxembourg City, Luxembourg." Marissa just stared at Max with huge, expressive eyes and said, "Wow!" under her breath. Max explained how the wealth they had for so many generations had now been invested here in the States because he had put his roots down here. He was no longer interested in spending extended periods of time in Europe.

Marissa expressed how they have painted a complete picture of each other's history and, therefore, will understand each other more completely. Max smiled and asked about their cinder block confines and what she had investigated thus far. She explained that she had traversed the perimeter, holding onto the walls several times. Her discoveries were minimal, being the laundry sink affording cold water. There were no windows or doors except the trap door Max was lowered from. He requested to see where the hatch was and asked if that single light bulb on the ceiling was the only illumination of their space. She shook her head affirmatively and then showed him the luxuries their captors had given them.

Further back, almost to the sink, stood a composting toilet with biodegradable toilet tissue. The sink, as previously stated, had only cold water. Although not ideal, there was shampoo and soap there, along with a toothbrush and toothpaste. Marissa stated she had no qualms about sharing if Max wanted to.

Marissa handed Max his pair of sweats to change into while describing her cleaning of their intimate sleeping space. She described dragging the mattress away from where it currently sits to attempt to rid it of as much dust as possible. She then walked to the far wall to shake out the cloth that held the package, finding it was actually another blanket. They could now experience the luxury of each having a blanket for sleeping. Enjoying the view of Max's tight-fitting sweats as he reached for the overhead pipe, she questioned what he had in mind. He asked her how much she liked her red silk dress. She looked puzzled when he explained if they tore it into strips, it could be used as a rope. She laughed and asked if he was thinking of Shibari Bondage at a time like this. He smiled and said no, but that he was up for whatever she wanted to do. Still chuckling, Max said, "If we could secure a rope to that pipe by the hatch and you could stand on my shoulders, we might just be able to open that hatch enough to grab the ladder for our escape." Marissa said, "Are you serious?" Max responded by pointing out he knows how flexible and athletic she is and is light enough to balance on his shoulders. It would be similar to him doing a deadlift with weights. He knew he could lift her up there, and the rope would support her, affording her some stability and something to hold on to for balance when he lifted her.

Marissa retrieved the dress and began tearing strips from it using her teeth to start the tears. Max watched enthusiastically. Grabbing the dress from her, he said, "I'll tear if you can braid the strips for strength." She retorted, "You don't know how to braid?" He smiled and responded, "That was not an elective course at Harvard." Smiling to themselves, they worked in silence for some time until they heard footfalls above their heads again. Max stuffed the dress and what they completed under the blankets on the mattress just as the hatch opened. Max walked over and stood under the hatch, looking up into Jonathan Abrams' face. Max questioned how long they were going to be kept captive and where exactly were they? He yelled at Abrams, "It won't matter if you even give me the address since we have no cell phone or way to get out!" Abrams just smiled and lowered a large bag of food down to Max's hands without the use of the ladder. Max was able to detect the configuration of the hatch and the area surrounding it while it was illuminated by the light from above. Max was disconcerted by the lack of visible walls or a finished ceiling on the floor above. This must mean they are in a warehouse-type building.

Once Abrams and his cohorts left, Marissa retrieved the dress pieces and went back to work. Max asked if she was hungry since it appeared they actually had a hot meal in the bag. Pulling the containers of Chinese takeout from the bag, Max triumphantly held up a plastic knife. His enthusiasm for such a trivial thing made Marissa more hopeful. Max identified the plastic knife as a perfect tool for shredding her silk dress. He continued removing containers from the bag, noting fried rice, mu shu pork, sesame chicken, lo mein, szechuan green beans and even fortune cookies, laughing. Marissa asked, "What's so Funny?" Causing Max to laugh louder declaring their fate may be described inside one of those cookies!

After consuming the takeout, Marissa commented that her meal could have been so much better with a glass of wine or saki. Max smiled at her comment but voiced his concern about not knowing how long this confinement would be. Marissa declared, "Not too much longer if your escape plan works!" Max asserted that if they could complete the rope tonight, they may be able to implement the plan in the morning after a good night's rest.

Wrapping Marissa in his arms as they stretched out on the Mattress together just felt natural, as did her head on his chest drifting off to the cadence of his heartbeat. As he kissed the top of her head, Marissa gazed up into Max's eyes and asked if he would relax better after they played a bit. He smiled and asked what she had in mind. She wrestled his shirt off, revealing his muscular upper body, and ran her hand down slowly over his abs, causing them to tighten with the feathered touch. Rising to her knees, she straddled his lap and raised his arms over his head. His fresh, woody perfume, mixed with a little sweat and his musky body odor, resulted in the sexiest of fragrances. Marissa smirked and whispered in a sultry voice, "Keep your arms there and close your eyes. Don't open them until I say so."

There was that smile of satisfaction as Max growled, "Yes ma'am. Your wish is my command." She then lowered Max's sweatpants, using them to tie his hands above his head. She then began kissing him under his ears and neck, and then proceeded to kiss his tied-up arms, starting from his forearms to inner biceps to his underarms, biting, licking, and smelling every inch of his body. Reaching his nipples, they puckered as goosebumps rose on his torso. By the time Marissa circled around and then inserted her tongue into his belly button, Max was growling and inviting her mouth to his quite prominent and visible erection. Passing by it with just a single stroke of her tongue had him moaning and writhing passionately. She continued slowly down his legs to his knees, massaging her way back up his muscled thighs and stopping to fondle his balls.

At this point, he opened his eyes and begged her to ride him to her completion. She laughed at his discomfort but was accommodating. Climbing slowly up his body, she stood over him to remove her sweatpants and then her top. He could see her arousal and was extremely grateful when she lowered herself to her knees, still holding his hands above his head. Riding cowgirl, building her pace slowly, she smiled down at Max, confirming her enjoyment. Rocking and rotating her hips as the speed increased, they both closed their eyes. Marissa threw her head back as she moaned her release. Max was right with her, groaning her name. She flopped down on top of him as he worked his hands free of his restraints and wrapped them around her, stroking her back and giving her butt cheek a quick slap. She raised her head to look up at him. Smiling, exposing dimples she hadn't noticed before, he declared, "You are such a tease!" She smiled and whispered, "And you love it!" He just uttered the one word "Yes" as they both succumbed to exhaustion.

When he opened his eyes on what he assumed was the following morning, he smiled at her naked body pressed against his. "I could get used to this," he mused. Stroking her hair from her face, he lowered his mouth to her lips and then to her breast, causing her to moan slightly. Slowly stroking his way to the apex of her thighs, he inserted one finger as she moved against him in the beginning of a rhythm. He promptly removed his hand and pulled her back to his chest as he entered her from behind. He was pumping into her slowly as she moaned, "This is not just a dream, right? I would enjoy waking up this way every morning!" With one hand cupping her breast and the other massaging her clit, he pinched her nipple, causing her orgasm to take over. Flipping her to her back, he entered her again and brought her to another as he found his release. Kissing her deeply, he ran his hands up and down her sides as he said, "Now, to work!" She murmured, "Slave driver!"

Removing his belt from his other pants he attached it to the silk rope they wove last night. After relieving herself and dressing, she moved towards him. He tried to toss the rope over the heavy pipe in the ceiling three times before he succeeded in getting it over. Tying it off and placing his belt around her waist, he explained how she would step onto his thighs as he squatted down and then climb to his shoulders. He would stand slowly while she steadied herself using the rope around the pipe. It only took two attempts for success. He planted his feet wide for balance, locking his knees as she placed her palms against the hatch. Pushing with everything in her, the hatch lifted several inches, but not enough to get her hand in to grab the ladder. As his knees began to wobble, he assisted her from his shoulders to the floor and cursed their failure.

Chapter 8

Arriving at Roger's townhouse at the break of dawn, Mark was armed with a million more questions. Surprised by Roger's awareness of his arrival, Mark stumbled back as the front door flew open. Roger didn't even allow Mark past the threshold before he blurted out that he now had the identity of the other two abductors. His software was able to pick up enough facial recognition to build a composite of the other two faces and identify them. Mark was impressed with that finding, but the revelry was cut short when the front door chimed again. Roger greeted Lionel with the same information, who then asked Roger to send this information to his tech people in order to get some apprehensions underway. Jonathan Abrams had evidently hired 20-year-old Tony Jacobson and his 28-year-old cousin, Marty Wentworth, to assist with the abduction plans.

After transferring all of the names, details and how the names were procured to the FBI's main tech office, the three men sat down to brainstorm. Lionel verified the information about the Gallery through Janet Mayfield. She was informed that Ms. Calloway decided on an impromptu trip to visit her father in Mykonos. Janet was stunned by this information because everything Marissa did was planned, calculated and documented.

Impromptu, where her gallery was concerned, just wasn't something she did. Janet explained that Marissa believed her success was based on a lot of planning. Janet also said that with Marissa gone, Jonathan had been keeping a very loose schedule at work. Lionel informed Janet that Mr. Abrams would be out of the gallery for an unforeseen amount of time, and Janet would have to hold down the fort. She smiled at him and responded with "No problem!"

Lionel informed the other two that once the names were handed over to the FBI, the three men suspected of the abduction should be apprehended quickly, Especially since they weren't even aware of having been identified.

Meanwhile, Lionel was just informed of a woman who was just picked up from Marissa's townhouse. She claimed to be a close friend and agreed to being transported to Roger's for questioning. Once she was led into the Brownstone, the first question from her mouth was, "Where is Marissa, and what is going on?" She appeared genuinely upset and close to tears! Roger offered her some coffee, to which she began to sob. She explained that she and Marissa have a standing Monday morning date at "The Witches Brew" coffee house in Georgetown. They would meet there every Monday at 7:30 a.m. and had since they were roommates at Wellesley College from Freshman year until they graduated. This was the first time Marissa missed a Monday other than when she let Maggie know she would be away. She told them they could verify all this information with the owner of the coffee house, "Gerty Williamson," who was a Wellesley alum also. Maggie then went on to explain that she went to Marissa's townhouse because she was afraid that something was terribly wrong after not having her phone calls answered. The message said her mailbox was full, and that would not be something Marissa would ever let happen! Regaining her composure, she asked if someone would please tell her what was going on.

Lionel asked if she knew anything about Marissa's relationship with her father. Hanging her head, she mumbled, "That hasn't been good since her mother died during her last year at Stanford, where she went for her Master's degree." Lionel then pressed with, "Explain not good to me, please." Maggie looked up and said, "Marissa hasn't spoken to her father for more than a year. When they did communicate before, it was very contentious. He didn't believe she could succeed on her own and was very controlling. He wanted her to be part of his import business and forgo her dreams. She has been very successful on her own without any financial backing or support from him."

Lionel had an agent go to "Witches Brew" coffee house to speak with Gerty Williamson. Once all of the details Maggie provided were verified, Lionel gave her a brief synopsis of what had been going on. She was devastated by the news of Marissa's abduction and dropped her head to the table, sobbing into her hands. Roger put his arm around her to comfort her until she again gained control of herself. Mark then asked, "Does Marissa have anyone in particular she has been dating?" Maggie reported that since her one steady boyfriend in her junior year at Wellesley, she had dated here and there but never anything serious. Mark then asked if any of them was questionable as far as stalking or not accepting Marissa limiting their social contact. Maggie again said, "Not that I know of. Marissa always was upfront with them that it was just a one-off for dinner or a show." then she reported matter of factly, "She satisfies her sexual appetite at Coeur Noir."

After Maggie's candid interview, Lionel had one of the agents take Maggie back home, satisfied with the information she gave and what he had verified. Looking over at Mark, Lionel said, "I was inside that club and was startled by parts of it. Please enlighten me so I am no longer being judgemental." Laughing, Mark described the club. "The club offers a secure environment to explore different sexual desires. There is a hefty membership fee and background check, which cuts down on any riff-raff, if you will. People can go to watch those that are exhibitionists, or reserve a room for a period of time to use a variety of toys within that room. Some members enjoy expanding their experiences in a sadistic way or masochistic way. Others just enjoy playing with different partners and toys within the room."

Lionel then wanted to know, "What kind of toys are we talking about?" Mark then described using blindfolds to enhance the sensory experience, handcuffs or rope to immobilize one of the partners as in bondage, Nipple clamps or cock rings to promote a more sensual orgasm, and whips, if you are into that sort of experience. Often, one of the suspension harnesses or swings aids the experience." As Lionel tried to take this all in, the thought then surfaced: "How do you choose a partner then?" Mark laughed again, saying, "It's very simple. You talk about what you are looking for with whoever you choose that night. If they aren't into what you want, you choose someone else."

Lionel then questioned, "And Marissa. What are her tastes?" Mark explained, "She has been the most desired woman at the club for some time. Men and women alike would love to have some time with her. She is adventuresome, agile and flat-out gorgeous, but does not participate in anything involving violence or great physical pain." Lionel then smirked, saying, "I think I have a clearer picture now." Roger then said Max had been trying to get him to join, and after hearing someone else extoll the benefits, he just might. Lionel then asked what the membership fee was. Mark said a hefty one-time $250 grand! Lionel whistled and said, "I can see the draw of that exclusivity! Certainly out of my league!"

Moving on to the next topic in question, Mark asked if Lionel would check to see if Jonathan Abrams, Tony

Jacobson and Marty Wentworth had been apprehended yet. He then questioned who would interview them and would any deals be negotiated in order to get one to tell where Max and Marissa were or who was actually calling the shots.

Lionel then grabbed his phone and contacted those sent to apprehend those men. Smiling, he said he would have to go to headquarters for a couple of hours to interrogate the three men who were identified.

Chapter 9

Spending at least an hour of brainstorming with no real plan in place for escape, Marissa and Max were feeling defeated. Marissa then ran her hand over Max's thigh, asking if his legs were sore from trying to balance her on his shoulders. He smiled and replied, "Nothing I can't handle." She smiled up at him as her eyes went dark and went to her knees in front of him, pushing his back to the mattress. She began by massaging his feet, then calves and stopped at his thighs. She then told him to roll over, and she would relax his back and shoulders. He did what he was told and moaned his gratitude as she worked massaging his neck, shoulders, down his back and to his tight, muscular buttocks. Grabbing her arms as he turned, she then fell to the mattress, giggling. He growled, "Too many clothes between us!" then, pulling his shirt over his head and discarding hers in a pile with his, he pulled her pants off and also tossed them. She smiled up at him and said, "Yours?" He immediately accommodated her. With both of them naked and aroused, a mixture of sounds and moans echoed through the cinder block confines as they chased their release. They then relaxed in a tangle of limbs and blankets.

Max chuckled, disclosing how that was very helpful in promoting relaxation! Marissa responded with a giggle and "Duly noted. Anytime I can help, just ask." He smiled with the retort of "Anytime?" She nodded in affirmation as they both drifted off for a while, still wrapped in each other's arms.

Max woke her as he removed his arm from under her and shook it out. She looked up at him quizzically. "Pins and needles," he said. Hearing voices above them then, Max grabbed their clothes and they hastily pulled them on. Suddenly, they heard "Over here!" and the hatch opened. Max pulled Marissa back into the shadows until they realized the legs they were seeing and the voices belonged to their rescuers. As that ladder was lowered, a man and a woman, wearing dark blue jackets emblazoned with the acronym FBI, descended. Introducing themselves as Tracey and Will, they moved over to check on Max and Marissa. Not wanting to spend one more minute in their dank, dark prison, Max said, "Let us get into the light above, and you can check us out and question us all you want."

As Marissa ascended the ladder, Max stood underneath her in case she faltered. Experiencing daylight for the first time in almost a week was an assault on the senses. Yet such a welcome sight. As Max set foot on the solid floor above their former confines, he hugged the person closest to him, saying, "How can we ever thank you? And, where the hell are we?" They all laughed and answered, "In Arlington, Virginia, about 15 minutes outside of D.C. as the crow flies. And just finding you both alive and healthy is all the thanks we need!" They were quickly bundled into one of those black SUVs and on their way to FBI Central. Max sat with his arm tightly around Marissa's shoulder as if he expected her to float away at any moment. She leaned into him and sighed, whispering to him, "Is this really over?" He squeezed her arm and whispered back, "Hopefully, yes!"

Arriving at the headquarters for debriefing, they drove in a caravan of SUV's into the underground parking. Pulling up to a large metal door, they were helped down as one agent keyed in the entry code. Max marveled at the depth of the bullet and probably bomb-proof door, rivaling those in bank vaults. Ascending to the 7th floor in the elevator, Max held Marissa's hand tightly. It seemed that personal contact was all that was grounding them both currently. When the doors to the main agent's desk area opened, there was a swell of applause, welcoming them back from their cinder block prison.

They were then ushered into a small, well-appointed room with sandwiches and drinks on a table, as well as cookies and a coffee carafe. Max smiled as he sank into a plush sofa, pulling Marissa down with him. Everyone's attention went to the door as Roger, Mark and Lionel walked through. Max jumped up, embracing Roger and shaking hands with Mark and Lionel. Marissa watched from her perch on the sofa, smiling. "I guess you know these people?" she mused to no one in particular as her response to the welcoming energy in the room. Max then introduced her to his best friend and "brother" Roger and the P.I., who was instrumental in finding them both. Marissa smiled at Mark and said, "I didn't think our next encounter would be under these circumstances!" To which they both laughed and Max put his arm around her again, obviously staking his claim. Lionel, the obvious head of the group of agents, asked if they wanted to eat something before the debriefing began. Max responded immediately with, "Coffee, please!" Marissa, smiling, asked, "Make it two?"

With cups in hand, Lionel directed his first questions to Marissa after keying up the cameras and recording equipment. She then launched into her recollection of events on that infamous Thursday night, leaving out the intimate details. She addressed the delivery of the champagne and truffles to the "Red Room" by someone she assumed was a new employee of the club. Then her recall became fuzzy, and she remembered kissing Max good night at the door sometime around 2:00 a.m. and locking it behind him. She assumed she cleaned up her "toys" as she always does, but couldn't remember actually doing it. She described how her vision was blurry, she was feeling warmer than usual, and the sounds were like noise underwater. The next recollection was waking to some sort of pounding noise overhead and the dank, musty mattress she was lying on. There was just a single bare bulb illuminating the space, and she was there wrapped in a threadbare blanket with nothing but her red silk dress on. She wore no undergarments or shoes, and all of her jewelry was missing. She recalled finding blood on her hands and dress, causing her to take stock of herself. She had not incurred any cuts, so she assumed it was from someone else. She then told the tale of her captivity in that cinder block and concrete enclosure. She went into detail about how her food was evidently laced with some drug to cause her intermittent lapses in consciousness. During these times, food and necessary supplies were delivered. She explained how she refused to eat or drink anything left for her the one day she finally glimpsed one of her captors, who she recognized immediately as her gallery manager for the past three years. A trusted employee betraying her was unfathomable.

She deferred to Max for the remainder of the time since that is when he was delivered to the confinement. Max concentrated on the time he spent thinking about Marissa on the drive to Roger's brownstone. He admitted that he was completely distracted by the thought of her being abducted right after his time spent with her. He was repentant for not offering her a ride home that night and vowed to make up for his guilt by tracking her down and rescuing her. So much so that he was paying no attention to his surroundings as he pulled up across the street from Roger's place. He said he recalls closing the door to his car and remembering his phone was still inside. As he turned around to retrieve it, a dark van pulled up next to him, and two men jumped out. The next thing he knew, he felt a prick to his neck, and his world went dark. He had no recollection of anything until he woke to find "Flame," a.k.a. Marissa, in front of him in a dark, dirty basement of some sort.

Marissa then detailed her experience and what she had found out about their cinder block prison, offering him something to drink and using acupressure to help dispel the pain in his head from whatever they had given him. He described their plan for an escape and how, even after all they had successfully accomplished, the plan ultimately failed. That took them up to the point where they heard the voices overhead and were retrieved from that hole by the agents. With that being said, Max questioned how they were found.

Lionel then took over the Narrative, chronicling the steps taken to apprehend the three men they believe were hired to pull off the abduction of both Marissa and Max. He then explained how offering a deal to the youngest man, who was believed to be the deliverer of the champagne to the Red Room, disclosed the location where they were being held. Lionel then showed a picture to Marissa of the younger man. Her response was a resounding "That's him!!!" With a questioning expression, she turned to Max and asked how it was that the champagne hadn't affected him. He smiled and stated sheepishly, "I am not a big fan of Champagne, so I just took that one small sip you offered and put the flute down, not to be picked up again." She blushed and admitted that she had at least 3 flutes of the bubbly. Lionel then disclosed that the opened bottle had been laced with Phenobarbital. The big question was still, why were they targeted and, ultimately, by whom?

Feeling drained and overwhelmed, Marissa requested a reprieve from any more questions today. She stated she would be more than happy to complete the debrief tomorrow, asking if it was safe to go home. Max suggested an agent drive them to her place to retrieve clothing and personal items and then drop them off at his penthouse, where they would be much more secure. Marissa acquiesced, stating she was uncomfortable even thinking about being alone at home.

Making their way back down to the garage with the male and female agent that Lionel suggested accompany them, they each took a relieved breath. Once at Marissa's home, Max suggested she pack a couple of days worth of clothing in case that was needed. Marissa didn't object at all, making Max smile internally.

The ride to Max's building was almost silent. The one agent said he would accompany them to Max's unit while the woman waited with the car. Once inside the building, Max directed him to the farthest bank of elevators and, using his thumbprint, opened the last elevator in the group. The agent raised an eyebrow, stating, "I guess you would feel secure here. Biometrics aren't normally used in residential buildings." Max said only in his elevator was it used. That afforded him the security he desired, so he had it installed personally.

When the door opened, Agent Franklin gasped and bluntly stated, "I get it now!" Thanking him for the escort, Max closed the elevator doors to afford him and Marissa the privacy they craved at this juncture. Marissa laughed and stated, "I wonder how that conversation back to the central building will go?" Max stated, "I would expect some professionalism on his part." And then Max asked, "Food or bath first?" Marissa smiled and said a bath would be divine. Max took her hand and guided her down the hall. Entering the primary bedroom, Max called out, "Close drapes, turn on ambient lighting." Both happened simultaneously! The ceiling took on the hue of a night sky as the striped velvet drapes swooshed across the expanse of glass. Marissa looked up at Max and exclaimed, "Nice!" Smiling, he directed her to the ensuite, where her bare feet experienced the marble floor heated to a comfortable 80 degrees. Continuing past the huge shower, he opened the doors to a sunken tub, where he flipped the switch, turning on the waterfall down the river rock into the four-person tub. He said he would allow her privacy unless she wanted company. She glanced at him from under long, thick eyelashes and conceded to whatever he would like to have happen.

Spinning her around and into his hard body, he reached for the hem of her sweatshirt to tug it over her head. He then smiled and stated that she may want some assistance in washing her hair and scrubbing her back. She just purred at him and took the bottom of his sweatshirt in her hands and tugged it up, revealing his abs and a smattering of hair across his pecs. Licking her lips, she reiterated that turnabout is always fair play. He smiled, stepped out of his sweatpants, and tugged hers down her legs. Lifting her up to wrap her legs around his waist, he took two long strides into the tub and sank into the heated water with a satisfied moan. She dropped her head back into the water, exposing that long neck and perfect breasts that he proceeded to take into his mouth. She voiced one word in that motion: "Delicious!" To which he just moaned, "Uh huh!" They luxuriated and played in the reheated water, washing every surface of each other's bodies for over an hour until she giggled that she was becoming a raisin.

He lifted her out and wrapped her in a heated bath sheet, carrying her to the bed. She stopped him by admitting, "I'm famished." He asked what she would like to eat. She smiled the smile of a vixen and said, "You silly!" He then tossed her onto the bed and climbed in as she bounced from the force of his throw. She wasted no time in working every bit of his body into a frenzy. When he couldn't take any more of her teasing, he reached into the side pocket of his robe and withdrew two sets of shackles. She smiled and asked, "Two?" to which he recited, "Hands at the top, feet at the bottom." She smiled and spread herself out into a perfect figure, "X". Marissa was now completely tied-up, with her arms behind her head and her legs spread out wide. She had never felt so naked and exposed, and she couldn't be more aroused for what was to come…

Hours later, flushed and completely satiated, they went to the kitchen to see what they could find. Max chopped some vegetables expertly and threw them into a preheated pan, developing a perfect brunoise. Then, cracking some eggs and whisking them over the heat, he asked, "Cheese or no cheese?" She smiled and responded, "Chef's choice!" He directed her to grab a bottle of wine from the rack and open it as he plated the omelet. Seated at the breakfast bar, they ate in comfortable silence. Placing the dishes in the sink, he stated the cleaning crew would take care of them in the morning. They then sauntered to the sofa to go over plans for the next day. Max asked if she wanted to continue the debriefing here or at Central tomorrow. She looked puzzled and said, "They would come here if we asked?" He said, "Whatever you want is what we will make happen." She smiled and purred, "Here then."

As the morning broke to the east, the only indication of it was the sounds in the kitchen. Marissa was startled awake and whispered, "Max, someone is in the condo!" He laughed and said it was the cleaning crew that he had let in an hour ago. She had slept so soundly that she hadn't even heard him get up. He smiled at her and said she could stay in bed as long as she wanted. Kissing him and laying her left leg and arm across his torso, he moaned and said don't tempt him when the day needs to get underway, and if he started working his way up her body, they would be here until at least noon. She giggled and whispered, "Raincheck?" He kissed her and tossed back the covers, exposing both her puckered nipples and his erection. They both moaned but started their morning in spite of themselves.

Chapter 10

Lionel got the call from Max to meet at his condo today for the remainder of the debriefing. He would have denied that request if it wasn't for the files they would have to go through today to find the main character in this abduction plot. He put a call in to his tech people to have the video and sound equipment transported to 601 Wharf St. S.W. They will all rendezvous in the lobby, so Max only has to come down once to take them up to the penthouse. Lionel thought it would be prudent to also call Roger and Mark to have them join the team there to be interrogated at the same time.

Arriving in the lobby, Roger was able to take them all upstairs using his biometric marker that was programmed in. Shooting Max a quick text to alert him to everyone's arrival, they all squeezed into the elevator. Lionel forgot to apprise his people of the "James Bond" style condo. So, when the doors opened, the gasps and curses under their breath could still be heard. Lionel chuckled to himself and turned, saying, "Just wait!"

Stepping out of the elevator, the first agent dropped his case of equipment and went directly to the expansive ceiling-to-floor glass window, observing the sun reflecting the surrounding buildings on the water. The Potomac was like glass this morning. The only thing disturbing the surface was a single sloop in full sail gliding at a gentle speed. The feeling of complete ataraxy overtook him for a moment until he heard Lionel talking to Max.

Everyone turned in unison as Marissa sashayed into the room wearing a floor-length, off-the-shoulder floral dress of a diaphanous fabric that seemed to float around her. Her bare feet, poking out as she walked, added to the thought of an angel in our company. Smiling, Max strode over to her and kissed her, staking his claim again. *I have to laugh at myself for my animalistic tendencies. What comes next, peeing on her to mark her as mine?*

With the video feed and taping of the narrative set up, they all sat at my dining room table to begin where they'd left off yesterday. Marissa and Max had ordered bagels and all the fixings earlier. They were delivered along with coffee, tea and cookies. With the food in the middle of the table, they began while munching on their breakfast spread. It was fun for them watching the two new agents that accompanied Lionel. They were introduced as Ken and Wayne. Wayne couldn't concentrate very long on our debriefing since his head kept pivoting to take in the room. Every so often, Ken would nudge him to return his focus. Max stifled his chuckling to maintain the business atmosphere in the room.

Mark described his interview with Janet Mayfield, Marissa's office manager and artistic display person. He intoned the same thing about Janet being an energetic and competent employee both times he interviewed her. He also described his interrogation of Bart, the bouncer and Gary, the Thursday night bartender from the club. The one thing he reported that none of us were aware of was Cyrus and Felix, the club owners, receiving an email from Mr. Calloway. Malcolm Calloway the 3rd, Marissa's estranged father, enquired about Marissa's club membership. Their response was that she was past the age of majority and was able to pay her fees on her own, and that was all they would convey about her to any outside individual. Marissa bristled at this invasion of her privacy and made a note to call him out about it.

Roger then described the day of my abduction from in front of his brownstone. He gave the partial Virginia tag he was able to read and the description of the men in his recollection. He then remembered something he had not yet reported. It seemed trivial at the time, so he let it slide. Seeing now that it may be pertinent, he explained how he picked up the "cupcake" Theresa Brown, whom he brought to his Friday night gathering, from in front of Marissa's townhouse. He then turned to Marissa asking if she was or ever had been a roommate. Marissa stated that she doesn't have and never would have a roommate. She claimed roommates caused too much drama and went on to report that her only real girlfriend was Maggie whom she has had since freshman year of undergrad at

Wellesley. Lionel jumped in to get any and all information Roger had about this young woman, thinking she may be another person to pick up for questioning. Roger then reminded Lionel about the two cryptic emails he and I had gotten from the library IP address. Lionel shook his head, saying they were a dead end.

Roger then disclosed that he, Mark and Lionel had gone through some of my case files after Max was abducted. Max's eyes shot up to lock onto Roger's, questioning the reason for that. Lionel interjected that they were trying to link Marissa's and Max's kidnapping to each other. He claimed any thread they could find was very important at that time. Showing Max the notes, he took about their findings caused Max to suddenly bolt to his home office. Lionel motioned for Ken to join him in following Max to the file cabinets in my office. Uncovering the concealed file drawers made Ken comment, "James Bond-esque from beginning to end!" Max smiled at that description but tore through the chronological case files in search of the cases he was called in on by the two law offices he did consultations for. Finding eight cases in less than ten minutes made him ill at ease. He carried the files into the dining area and laid them in front of him.

Opening each file and immediately finding his report about Shell companies filing injunctions or Lawsuits against Calloway Galleries made his heart pound loud enough that he was sure everyone in the room could hear it. Max looked up at Marissa and remarked that he was able to block any injunctions and help win the lawsuits with the information I uncovered. She smiled and said, "My attorneys handled everything. I never even wanted to have any information other than I lost or won! I had enough going on without adding that stress. That's why I paid them the big bucks!" With that, she reached over and squeezed his hand, whispering under her breath, "Thank you."

After pondering the outcomes and putting some of the background in perspective, she looked up and asked, "And... these shell companies, were they ever traced to a business or a person?" To which Lionel replied, "Your father!"

Marissa shot up from the table and paced back and forth in front of the window. She was muttering under her breath, "That son of a bitch! That lousy misogynistic, narcissistic old man! He always tries to ruin everything!" "He will get his! I'll see him imprisoned if it is the last thing I do!" Max told her, then walked over and wrapped her in his arms. Turning to those at the table, he said, "Give us a few minutes, please." Walking her back to the bedroom, she began to relax a bit.

They sat on the bed with Max's arms still around Marissa and her head on his chest. Her breathing began to slow to a more normal rate as he asked her to share her feelings with him. Adjusting herself on the bed, she took his hands in hers and looked up at him, saying, "There is a backstory that I had filed away a long time ago…"

With her head down, she recanted the story of her youth. As she had described before, her father was infrequently around. When he was, though, he had violent outbursts that she was the recipient of. He would find fault with any number of things. She was a straight-A student most of the time. She occasionally would get a B+ in English or one of the foreign languages she took. If he was around when that report came in, he would take the strap to her, but not just anywhere. He would find an area that would not be visible to the public and beat her until she bled. If he wasn't satisfied with that punishment, he would lock her in the wine cellar and extinguish the light. She recalled sitting on the floor with her knees to her chest, pulled up as tightly as she could and crying. She was terrified of rats and mice and could either hear or feel them scurrying past her feet. Her time in confinement was whatever suited him. She remembered being locked down there during a house party for hours until a staff member was sent down to replenish the bottles that had been consumed. When she snuck upstairs to bed, she was yanked out by her hair by her livid father after the party. He proceeded to lock her up overnight that time. With tears streaming down her face, Marissa recalled him telling her he would never help her set up any type of business, especially related to something like art. If she refused to go for her master's in business and work for him, he would ruin her! "So, there you have it…the crux of our relationship!"

Max's eyes welled with tears as he kissed her and told her he would be there anytime she needed him, for any reason. Then he proceeded to pull her dress down, exposing her nipples and taking each into his mouth, nipping at them until she moaned. He then pulled up the skirt of her dress and knelt in front of her. Pulling her legs over his shoulders, he moved the fabric of her thong out of the way as he buried his face between her thighs. He licked and sucked in circles, occasionally darting his tongue inside, until she finally orgasmed twice, shaking and writhing in pleasure each time. Rising, he went into the ensuite, washed his face and brought her a warm towel, stating, "Now, I think you feel well enough to go back out to the living room." She stood and kissed him, stating, "I will reciprocate later." He smiled and answered, "Yes you will!" as he took her hand to guide her into the hall.

Once settled back at the table, it was obvious to everyone that Marissa had been deeply emotional after the revelation of the files. Her eyes were rimmed in red, as well as her nose. But they still needed to follow up on her father's possible involvement. Max stated, "Suffice it to say, Malcolm Calloway is involved up to his eyebrows as far as I can see, and we will follow the trail, which is my specialty, until we have enough evidence to convict him!" With that, Roger smiled and said, "Amen!"

Max asked if pizza would be adequate for lunch as, in turn, all at the table refreshed themselves in the hall bathroom. Feeling as though it would be an appropriate time, he uncorked a bottle of Sangiovese Red and took it along with water to the table. When everyone had eaten their fill, they filed into the office again. Putting the files back in chronological order, Max closed the camouflaged file cabinet, eliciting another "Wow" from Wayne. Lionel asked if he could step out on the balcony for a few moments. He just felt the need for some fresh air. Of course, Max was amenable. He even suggested they move to the party deck on the roof and talk there for a change of scenery. Making their way down the hall, Wayne kept asking about the different photos. Roger said, "All previous or current clients." Wayne was in awe every step of the way. Lionel would have to remind him, once in the car, that he cannot divulge any information or describe his experiences today, even to office friends.

As they passed through the primary bedroom, they ascended the stairs through another concealed panel, revealing the rooftop deck and helipad. Max stepped over to the built in bar and opened the two refrigerators, offering for everyone to help themselves. Max sat on the wicker loveseat next to Marissa, who had gathered her feet under her and leaned into Max. There was a long wicker sectional and two extra swivel chairs around a huge cocktail table to accommodate them all. Wayne couldn't help himself and had to ask, "All of that artwork in the bedroom was real, right?" Max laughed and stated, "Originals that my parents had collected before their death. Before you ask any further questions, let me make something clear. I am a very private person and expect to never hear a word about what you have seen today. Yes, my life has been privileged, but I also work very hard! So, anything else you would like to ask, do it now, and then that is over, understood?" Wayne turned an amusing shade of crimson as he said, "Totally understood! I'm sorry, it's just that your life is something I would imagine most people only read about! Out of my league, no matter how many years I work!" Max then threw his head back and laughed. He then educated those who didn't know by stating, "My family was 6th generation wealth in Milan, Italy. They are now gone, and I am the only one left alive. So, what you see is my inheritance."

From that point on, the discussion went to the men being held by the FBI and what the next steps should be. Max voiced concern about the security At Marissa's townhouse. Roger offered to send his team over and outfit the place with state-of-the-art biometrics and cameras to up her security. He suggested using thumbprint-operated window locks from the inside and reinforced entry doors. Marissa asked if all of that was really necessary. Max turned using his courtroom baritone voice, saying, "Absolutely!"

She sighed and acquiesced. She knew she would sleep better knowing that security was in place. Roger said, "The equipment is yours. You just have to put up with a mess for a day!"

"A day?" she questioned. He nodded and said he has a large tech installation team. The only problem is they consider clean, removing the garbage afterward. She laughed and said, "No problem, cleaning can be cathartic... for the cleaning crew." They all laughed at that statement and moved on to the next topic. Tracking down her father.

The conversation seemed to lighten as the day disappeared. And one by one, the team departed just before dinner. Max asked if Marissa wanted to go out for dinner or order in. She put her head in his lap and threw her legs over the arm of the loveseat. Gazing lovingly up into Max's face, she asked if he would mind staying in. He groaned, "under one condition." She smiled and moaned, "My thoughts exactly. How private is it up here?" His response was, "Mine alone." So, Marissa turned and unzipped Max's slacks as she slid to her knees in front of him. He closed his eyes and enjoyed the night.

Chapter 11

After enjoying a very physical night, both Max and Marissa moaned when his phone sounded, slicing through the silence. She grabbed his hand before he reached for it and said let it go to your mailbox. We can check it later. Max reached over and ran his hand up her leg to the junction of her thighs, saying, "In that case, since I'm awake now." She growled, "You're insatiable." But when he touched her "on" button, she was on top of him instantly. He smiled and said, "I thought you were still tired." She said, "I did too!" They both laughed as she stroked his morning wood, eliciting a growl and a brisk turn where she was now on her back. He plunged deep and said, "This is going to be hard and fast! I was dreaming about this when the phone rang, and I don't think I can hold back." She giggled and said, "Let's see what you've got, big guy!" And then she moaned as he went even deeper, putting her right leg over his shoulder and hitting that perfect angle. The sound of the phone rang out again as Max yelled, "NOT NOW!"

Twenty minutes later, after catching their breath, Max listened to his voicemail. Watching his face morph into a scowl, she questioned his reaction. He said it was Lionel with some extremely important information. He is already on his way over. Max dialed his number and told him to stop at "Witches Brew" and pick up two black Colombian coffees and a couple of chocolate croissants if they were warm. They would be decent by that time. Lionel laughed, saying, "Oh, to be young and in love!" It took Max's breath away hearing that. He really was falling in love with this redhead! This is a first for him, and if Lionel hadn't said it, he would have denied it to himself!

Getting the call from the lobby security desk, Max threw shoes on to let Lionel up while Marissa finished dressing. Lionel entered the elevator as Max shot him a questioning look. Lionel said not until you are both seated, but I did get breakfast. Putting plates and napkins on the table as well as cream and sugar, Max was caught off guard when Lionel murmured, "Holy Mother…" Max turned to see Marissa in a hot pink sheer jacket over a black cropped bustier and short leather capris that looked like they had been sprayed on. This time, she had on hot pink sandals to coordinate, and her hair was braided over one shoulder with soft whisps floating around her fresh face, adorned with only mascara and lip gloss to match her jacket. Lionel turned to Max and said, "No wonder you were still in bed when I called. If I had that in my bed, I'd never get out!" Max laughed and joked, "Watch it, old man!"

Marissa sat down at the table and thanked Lionel for picking up coffee and croissants. She tucked in and reached across, saying "I'm famished", grabbing a croissant on a plate and dressing her coffee with cream only. They were both staring at her when she looked up and said, "What?" Max stated that Lionel wouldn't enlighten him until they were both seated. Lionel grabbed a coffee and began by clearing his throat. He then addressed Marissa. Your Father has been on our radar for a couple of days now. She nodded her understanding, saying, "And?" He is now on Interpol's radar too. Her eyebrows shot up to her hairline with shock. "Interpol? What for?" He then told her that Jonathan Abrams had received a wire transfer of a large sum from a Swiss bank account that has now been tied back to one of the Shell companies that we uncovered. And… interpol sent agents to your father's villa in Mykonos. Marissa held her breath, waiting for what came next. When entering the villa, after being let in by the help, they were handed a large manilla envelope. Inside was the deed to the property and a bank book with a substantial sum of money in the account. Both had been transferred into your name in the past week. A full year's salary was also transferred to the cook, maid, gardener and maintenance crew. But your father is now a ghost! He just disappeared. We were hoping you would have some insight.

Marissa slowly chewed her croissant as you could see the thoughts churning in her head. Looking up, she said he has a Lear jet and helicopter at his disposal. He can't fly the jet but he is licensed for the chopper. He has a lot of international contacts, too. I can't remember the names off the top of my head, but I must have them in a file at the gallery. I can dig those out for you, but as I said the other night, I haven't spoken to that man for over a year, and that was a very contentious conversation. I believe I may have told him to "F" himself as I slammed the phone down. So, I don't know how much help I am going to be.

Lionel then sadly addressed her, "Marissa, I am concerned for your safety with him going off the rails!" Max looked up and pleaded with her to stay here with him until this was settled. She agreed, saying she didn't think she would be able to sleep in her townhouse again until he was caught. I don't know what his long game is but it scares me just talking about it. He is the only other person with access to my home. Max responded reassuringly, saying that would change as soon as Roger's team installed her security system. Speaking of which, Marissa declared, how does that operate if there is no electricity? Max then smiled and told her that the system has a self-contained power source fed by solar and/or wind! But she would still be safer here with him! Lionel smiled and said, "Why don't we go together to your townhouse now, and you can pack up as much as we can carry and get you settled here with "Loverboy!" Max choked on that reference, but smiled in spite of himself.

The entire ride to her townhouse was tense for Marissa. She pressed her body against Max's, trying to draw some strength from his nearness. She has never been "the damsel in distress type". Her independence and self-assuredness were faltering, and that made her feel unstable. Without even realizing it, her tears were sliding down her cheek and onto Max's shirt. He grabbed her chin between his thumb and index finger and turned her face towards his. With a look of deep concern, he gently placed his lips on hers and said, "It's all going to work out! One foot in front of the other until we get there!" She tried to smile up at him, but it wasn't successful. He dropped his arm over her shoulder with his hand resting on her left breast. She moaned, and he responded with, "Now, there's my girl!" she swatted at him and began to laugh. He said, "That always seems to be effective in redirecting your attention." She checked on Lionel's eyes in the rearview mirror before she grabbed Max's thigh and worked her way up and over the zipper of his jeans, stroking out a groan. She then whispered in his ear, "Turn around is fair play," as she ran her tongue around the shell of his ear. He looked over at her with a smirk and those molten eyes, and she knew she would soon be in trouble.

Entering her townhouse felt alien to her. Would this ever feel like home again? She climbed the stairs to her bedroom with Max right behind her. He wasn't letting her out of his sight. She asked him to grab her suitcase from the top of the hall closet as she pulled hangers full of clothes from the closet. She tossed shoes into her tote bag as he sat on her bed and took in the very feminine vibe of her bedroom. The dove gray walls were accented by pale blush sheer curtains at the front window under a gray scalloped valance and velvet over drapes. The duvet was the same shade as her sheers, and the head of the bed was overflowing with soft tufted pillows in all shapes and sizes, giving the bed a soft, billowy feel. The mirrored nightstands reflected the beautiful crystal chandelier above the bed. The huge filigreed mirror on the opposite wall would offer quite a view of bedroom activities, were this room used for that. Somehow, Max doubted that Marissa ever brought anyone here to her sanctuary, though.

Max had slipped his shoes off upon entering the room, sinking his toes into the ultra-plush, soft gray carpeting. His fantasy would be to enjoy rolling around naked on the surface. His thoughts must have been read as Marissa pulled him to the floor and climbed onto his lap. She smiled and said, "Some other time since I had the same thought." "It's a shame we didn't come alone. It would be the christening of my space. You are the first man to ever step foot in here!" He smiled at that admission!

She then entered the ensuite and began filling another tote with all her makeup and toiletries. He came up behind her, wrapping his arms around her again from behind. He whispered in her ear that anything she would need, he could have delivered by the evening. She smiled at him in the mirror and said "Let's go then."

Downstairs, Lionel was taking stock of the easily accessed windows and counted the people walking around the neighborhood. The cobblestone streets out front added a touch of history to the area. Smiling as they came down the stairs carrying enough baggage for an extended holiday, he quipped, "Ready?" Marissa surveyed her domain one last time for a while and agreed "Ready."

When back on the road, Max suggested the three of them go to the Gallery and allow Marissa a few moments to go through her files. She would be able to dig into the past paperwork to see if she could find the names and places where her father may have connections that would hide him. Lionel heartily agreed that would make sense. Just as they turned onto the street where the gallery stands, Lionel got an important phone call. He was linked in on a conference call with his contact at Interpol.

Leaving Lionel in the car for some privacy, Max assisted Marissa from the Back seat. When they entered the Gallery, Janet Mayfield looked up from her work and ran to embrace Marissa. "Oh my God! I didn't know if I would ever see you again!" she exclaimed as she began to cry. Marissa gave her a brief synopsis of events and explained how her time in the gallery for the next couple of weeks would be limited. She would now be accessible by phone, though. I stepped in and gave Janet my card in case she couldn't reach Marissa. Introducing me to Janet was eye-opening. Marissa introduced me as the alternate attorney who saved her gallery and as her boyfriend.

Once in the back office, I confronted Marissa, asking, "Boyfriend?" She smiled and said, "You don't like that label?" My response was, "Very much, but we haven't spoken about what and where we are." She chuckled and said, "We will later. After all, I will be living with you. Right?" I just nodded affirmation, pointing to the file cabinet. Marissa went directly to the bottom drawer, explaining that all things Papa were in there. She pulled out a large file actually labeled contacts. She handed me a legal pad and asked me to record the names and places as she read through the papers. The first name was in London, Reggie Blacksmith. A moment later, she said Tokyo, then spelled out Haruto Tanaka. She frowned at the next sheet, saying she only had the place recorded. Bucharest, with no name associated with it in the file. "That's odd!" she murmured. That was followed quickly by Minsk. Again, she spelled out Alexander Ovechkin, recalling he was a more recent contact. Next was Tehran. When she spelled Hussein Gaffari, I did a double-take. I knew that name. But how and why? Lastly, she said again, I'll spell Donghyun Jeong from Seoul, South Korea. She then declared that if she had to guess, she would say put an asterisk next to Seoul and Minsk.

As she closed the file drawer, Lionel opened the outer door to the gallery. He made his way back to us in maybe ten strides, nodding to Janet as he passed. He looked like a man on a mission! He stepped into the office and immediately proclaimed that Interpol locked all of the accounts that they found attached to your father's name. Marissa looked up and stated, "He used to stash funds in Switzerland, the Caymans, and had a safe at the villa in Mykonos that I knew of." "My mother's jewelry was also locked in that safe!" He smiled and asked if we would be interested in a trip to the Greek Isles any time soon. Marissa blanched and divulged her disdain for that villa. Looking at me, she revealed that was the house with the large wine cellar and where her parents would throw lavish and raucous parties. "Not somewhere I want to go back to anytime soon!" Lionel then looked at her and asked, "Isn't that the house he just bequeathed to you?" She turned with an icy gaze saying, "Yes, and he knew it would disturb me! That's Why."

Chapter 12

Max

Lionel left us in the lobby of my building after helping unload Marissa's luggage. We ascended in the elevator with only the sound of our breathing. Walking back into my penthouse, I could see Marissa's shoulders relax and her face soften. Seeing how the events of the day affected her, I suggested a soak in the tub and a glass of wine. She looked at me, declaring, "You always know just what I need!"

We disrobed and climbed into warm water with the waterfall flowing in the background. I added Oil of Myrrh and lit a few candles around the room, turning off the overhead fixture. Leaning back and resting against my chest, she sighed and sipped her wine. She turned her head to speak to me over her shoulder. "There was a question of what our label should be earlier today." Smiling and kissing the top of her head, I explained, "You, my love, would be my first girlfriend if that is what we are!" She laughed and declared, "You have been more withdrawn than me!" I chuckled with, "Not celebate, but never found anyone to risk a relationship on! Until now, that is." Her hand slid up my thigh, slipping it behind her back and finding my reaction, she declared, "My feelings exactly! Are we exclusive then?" Smiling as wide as I ever had, my response was immediately and enthusiastically, "Exclusive it is! I like knowing you are all mine!" Her response was flipping over and sliding down my torso to land at that magic place with her thighs on either side of mine, declaring, "And... you are all mine!"

Rolling her hips on mine, in adagio time, she drove me wild. Not being able to position our bodies as I needed, I lifted her from the water as she squealed. We went no further than to the bedroom doorway, when I had to be inside her again. Lying her on the rug on her back, with her breasts heaving and her eyes locked into mine, I held her feet to my chest as I put my tip on her lips down under, rubbing my manhood on her clit. Once I had her begging me to put it all in, I slid all of my length into her warmth. She moaned, "Finally! Yes! Right there! Harder, please!" I was only too happy to accommodate! We both moaned each other's names as I shivered with the strongest release I had ever experienced. She held onto me for some time, sealing the connection before we finally pulled apart and rose to our feet. I smiled and presented the prospect of using every surface in the condo before the week was over. She giggled, responding with, "Maybe two weeks?" I murmured, "Give me ten minutes and a drink, and we can find another surface." Swatting my butt as she walked by, she smiled over her shoulder and asked, "Ten minutes? Really?" I ran after her then, throwing her over my shoulder and smacked her bottom as we entered the closet.

I pointed at the center case in the closet. "That is our next rendezvous spot!" She giggled and said, "Who is going to wash off the ass print when we are done?" Laughing, I replied, "No one! It will be another art installation! My first attempt." She looked at it again and implored me to consider a surface that wasn't glass. Keeping her over my shoulder, I paraded out of our bedroom and marched us naked down the hall.

When I reached the kitchen counter, I deposited her butt on the cold surface, soliciting a squeal. She leaned back, giving me a mental picture of what the next tryst would be. I opened the fridge and pulled out a bottle of vodka and the Amarena wild cherries. Her eyes widened as I opened the jar. Taking a plump cherry from the glass jar, I deposited it on her navel. Giggling uncontrollably, the juice escaped its confines and dripped down her hip. I chastised, "Now look what you've done," as I leaned over to lick the spill. Next, I poured a vodka shot and pushed her to her back as I cradled it between her breasts. Placing my lips on her nipples, I sucked, then nipped, working my way to the center when I picked the shot glass up with my mouth, tilted my head and pounded it back. I poured another one and repeated the process. Only, this time, I didn't swallow. Instead, I leaned over and put my mouth on hers, letting the liquid seep into her mouth. As she swallowed, I ran my tongue down her center to her navel and slurped the cherry from its perch.

Thinking I was done, she began to rise. Shaking my head no, I turned and retrieved an ice cube from the dispenser and ran it seductively around her nipples, then followed down the center of her ribcage until I reached her navel again. Instead of stopping there, I continued my path to her vulva. She shivered as I inserted what was left of the cube into my mouth and then ran my cold tongue up and down her center until she was writhing. When she appeared to be ready to explode, I stopped and smiled down at her. She grabbed my head, pulled me into a deep, sensuous kiss and moaned, "Don't stop now please. Take me!" Lifting her from the counter, I carried her to the sofa and continued my journey, licking and biting her thighs. When she seemed beyond aroused, I threw her left leg over my shoulder and again plunged deeply into her. She shook with an almost immediate orgasm as she called to me to keep going and never stop! I then flipped her to her stomach and raised her butt into the air, and pounded out my release as I strummed her clit. She screamed her simultaneous and explosive release just as the phone from the lobby security desk sounded.

Looking angrily at the phone as if that would silence it, we both burst out laughing. She questioned, "Do your friends turn up uninvited often?" I shook my head and answered the call. Security announced a visitor: a Mr. Lionel Sharpe was requesting to be allowed up. I told Dan, the night guard, to put him on the phone. Lionel said, "Can you let me up?" I told him it better be a life or death situation, to which he laughed and said "Sorry." I told him to give me a few minutes. He again laughed and apologized.

Throwing on a pair of jogging shorts and a T-shirt, I turned to see Marissa in a camisole and short shorts. Handing her one of my t-shirts, I said this may be better coverage since it's Lionel. She looked down, realizing her perky nipples were on full display through the silky Cami, and she pulled my shirt over her head.

After retrieving Lionel from the lobby, he immediately went to the counter with the paperwork that he said needed an immediate signature from Marissa. He looked down, recognizing the ass imprint in cherry juice on the counter, blushed slightly, and strode to the dining table. Clearing his throat, he claimed, "We can sign this more easily over here." Shooting me a knowing smirk, he went on to explain. "Interpol faxed these papers over that needed to be signed by Marissa right away. They are release forms for entrance into the Mykonos villa and access to the bank account that was signed over to you." She looked up and asked why. He looked puzzled and said, "Why what?" "Why do you need my permission to access this stuff now?" Marissa asked. Lionel then explained, "The cagey bastard transferred a bundle to the account with your name on it, thinking we wouldn't be able to freeze that. We want to transfer it to an account here in the States in your name. That way, he will have no access to the funds!" Marissa told him to freeze it indefinitely here until he was caught. "She has no need for the money and would love to have some means of vengeance against the old man!" Smiling, he said, "You've got it, sweetheart!" We all kind of chuckled and bid each other a good night.

Riding Lionel back down in the elevator, he smiled and said, "Sorry to have disturbed your creative play." I shot him a look that said, "Drop it," as he raised his hands in submission and coughed out, "Glad someone is enjoying life!" I told him we would touch base with him tomorrow as he left the building.

Turning around to go back upstairs, I caught a glimpse of a man across the street staring at us inside. The hairs on the back of my neck bristled as I turned to Dan and suggested he lock the exterior doors and just buzz those in that should be allowed in for the rest of the night. He smiled and said, "Will do Mr. Corleone." I then went back up to our secure little nest.

Seeing my expression when I came back in, she asked if there was something else wrong. I told her about the man watching from across the street and how my body immediately reacted. She kissed me and asked, "But, we're safe here, right?" I smiled and reassured her that we were protected by the best security available. And thought to myself *I happen to be an excellent marksman. But no one needs to know that.* Also, my glock was in a concealed drawer at the base of my bed.

We crawled into bed, leaving our clothes at the foot. She climbed onto my lap and smiled as she kissed and nipped her way down my body. We exchanged positions several times, imploring each other for release, before we were both exhausted and completely satisfied. Lying with her head on my chest, she fell asleep to the beat of a very contented heart! I mused as I drifted off, "This could be it for me. I could live like this forever!" Shivering at that declaration, I held her to me even tighter.

Chapter 13

Marissa

Walking into the Coeur Noir Club on a Thursday night at 9:30 again felt liberating. Passing by Bart, who was watching over the front door, winking at him and smiling as he whistled his approval, did something to my heart rate. Again, the coat check room was empty; it began feeling like Dejas Vu! Slinking into the main bar area in this form-hugging black leather strapless dress with sky-high heels garnered quite a few stares. My hair, in beachy waves, was caught on the right side with a shiny silver hair comb, baring my right shoulder to the cool air blowing from the ceiling vent above the bar stool I paused behind. The black lace choker I wore with the diamond drop earrings and tennis bracelet accented the dress perfectly, catching a few more eyes when the lights reflected on them. Nodding to Gary, Thursday night's mixologist, he smiled and placed my bourbon on the napkin in front of the gentleman's seat, voicing, "Looking good, Flame!" Smiling coyly, I asked if the Red Room was ready for me. As I scanned the tables around the room, there were several expectant faces hoping to be chosen. I blew a kiss to the 6'3" tall gentleman in the bespoke suit and Italian loafers at the end of the bar. He stood, taking his drink with him and strode over to the observation window.

When I stepped up next to him, he blew warm air on the right side of my neck, causing me to shiver and goose flesh to erupt on my arms. "Still so responsive," was the comment under his breath.

Just then, the Silver Fox stepped up on my other side, smiling. "Are you up for a threesome tonight, gorgeous?" he growled into my ear, just loud enough for those around us to hear. As I ran my hand down the lapel of his jacket and grabbed the arm of the 6'3" hunk, we made quite a show of walking to the Red Room and unlocking the door. I stepped inside, flipping on the light and adjusting it to my chosen setting. I proceeded to pull each man in behind me slowly and deliberately. As the door shut and locked, I blew out a deep breath. I looked at the two men as I whimpered, "Do you think they all bought that?" Max and Mark both chuckled and said, "You sold it well! Now we just need to wait."

Mark commented, "We could always play while waiting," to which Max responded, "Those days are over. You lost your chance, old man." Pointing between Max and me, he commented, "The only playing from here on out is exclusively between the two of us." With that, he palmed my ass and kissed me passionately. I then reached into the cabinet, dislodging the crop from the wall and snapped it into my palm twice while smiling. Max grinned and responded with, "We could play a little while waiting," as he grabbed the crop from me and ran it up my thigh, catching the hem of my dress and lifting it a few inches. Mark coughed and smiled in acknowledgment. He then opened his laptop on the bed and pulled up the camera feeds on a split screen. Staring at the screen and waiting was brutal. Mark again reiterated that it may take a couple of times before we snare the other man hired in an attempt to get to me.

By midnight, I was practically asleep with my head in Max's lap, when Mark yelled here we go! Caught on camera was a man and woman working on the door, trying to bypass the locking mechanism. Mark hit the button on his phone, and we watched two agents walk up behind them and escort them out the back door and into the FBI vehicle parked there. We stayed in that room for another half hour, watching the screen. Mark then packed up his laptop and said he would talk to us tomorrow as he left.

Max locked the door again, saying we shouldn't waste the entire evening. Pulling my dress zipper down and watching the butter-soft leather puddle on the floor, Max grinned at seeing me totally naked underneath and remarked that he preferred me wearing nothing under that skin, pretending to be a dress. I then queried, "Did you consider going commando tonight?" Max smiled as he first removed his socks and toed off his shoes, next were his jacket, then shirt. He put his hand on his zipper when I demanded he stop there. Dropping to my knees in front of him, I theatrically lowered his pants zipper using my teeth, making him harden immediately. Rising,

I asked if he wanted to choose first. He immediately walked to the Saint Andrews Cross, where I would be restrained in a spread-eagle position. I smiled and said, "OK. I want an adjustable cock ring, one that encircles the penis and balls. Have you ever tried one?" Max shook his head no as he looked at me with terror on his face. I explained that it makes the orgasm much more intense and can be released immediately with the locking button if it becomes uncomfortable. Max then sighed and relented. I put the ring on him and adjusted it for his comfort, then I stepped up to the Cross and asked Max to fasten the restraints. As he finished attaching my last hand, I looked down. He was more than ready. He began teasing my body with the crop that was still lying out. I called out, "No fair!" He laughed and continued to run it up and down my legs to the apex of my thighs.

He then circled my breast until he reached my nipples. Giving them a light flick of the crop, I pleaded, "Harder!" He then did it again a little harder as I moaned in pleasure. He saw I was completely aroused as the juices dripped down my leg. He then came up to me and adjusted the cross to the perfect height as he plunged into me. I was captive and unable to really move, which made Max that much more aroused. He was working up a sweat when I couldn't hold back anymore. He released the ring as we both went over the edge, screaming each other's names. After catching his breath, he removed the restraints, assisting me to my feet. Smiling, he asked how much a cross would be to install in his home gym. I grinned that evil grin and said several different C-rings are much easier to hide in a drawer. He responded with one word: "Dildo. I want to make you come with a dildo, too," were his whispered words.

Dressing for our departure, Max asked if I recognized the woman in the video tonight. I told him, "She doesn't look like anyone I knew. Why?" He said he was almost positive she was the young woman who accompanied Roger to his own party that Friday after my abduction. My eyes must have given my shock away as he continued to report that she was picked up by Roger from in front of my townhouse that evening. That was why they questioned me about having a roommate. I expressed my fears of this web becoming more expansive by the day. Max said, "You'll be safe staying with me," as he hugged me, kissing the top of my head.

We both were feeling a little paranoid as we walked to his car. Looking over his shoulder, Max unlocked my door, and I stepped in. He proceeded to circle the car, looking at the undercarriage and feeling the inside of the wheel wells. As he got in, seeing my expression, he explained that he just wanted to be especially careful.

Pulling into the underground secured garage, we both let go of the breath we hadn't realized we were holding. Max looked at me, shifting his position, and inquired, "How far do you believe your father is willing to go? And do you have any idea of his end game?" I just shrugged as a tear escaped my eye. Max wiped it with his thumb, saying, "We'll be OK!"

We dropped our shoes at the door and entered the penthouse. Max grabbed me around the waist, pulling me against his body. Whispering his query in my ear, "Bath or Shower?" I smiled and replied, "Shower! I want to watch my fears swirl down the drains." "Shower it is. I'll grab some fresh towels," he uttered as he walked down the hall.

The ensuite shower was like standing in the rainforest in the rainy season! We washed each other slowly until we couldn't restrain ourselves. Hands and fingers expertly worked for long moments until the animal instincts took over. Max took me against the wall of glass, hard and fast, expressing the need for our electric connection before we fell into the plush master bed. I smiled again, declaring, "I will never deny you!"

I slept like the dead, only waking when I moaned to Max's ministrations under the covers between my thighs. He was an early riser, that I knew. Giggling at my double entendre to myself, my silliness morphed into intense pleasure!

Chapter 14

Marissa

Since it was Friday, I suggested to Max that we do frozen Friday! He looked at me quizzically as I explained, after looking places up on the internet, how we should go all over D.C. and sample frozen treats all day. He laughed, saying he had never heard of that before. I countered, "Of course not. It was something my mother and I would do when I was a child in New York City." He questioned whether D.C would even hold a candle to N.Y.C when it came to frozen delicacies. Then questioned whether we should drive or chopper to New York to do it there. The thought was tempting, but would it be a security risk? Max said before we discount the idea, let him speak with Lionel.

When Max came sauntering down the hall, I could tell by his face that it was not going to happen. But then he looked up with that mischievous expression and disclosed that he already had Roger picking up at least a dozen flavors of ice cream and as many fixings as he could find. He would let Mark know, and we should call Maggie. "We'll have a frozen Friday party on the upstairs terrace! If you would like, you can also invite Janet Mayfield if you don't mind her closing the Gallery early," was his final suggestion.

Going to the bar, Max began pulling bottles from the cabinet. When I asked what he was doing, he snickered like a naughty child. "We are going to make this an adult-frozen Friday!" was his retort. "Grab the glasses for frozen daiquiris, margaritas, pina coladas and put them on the tray on the counter. I'll grab the blenders and any frozen fruit from the freezer. Hopefully, Roger will have some sherbet in his choices, and we can make spiked fruit slushies." "Just hope when we are done, everyone can make it back down the steps!" I laughed as Max carried an armful of bottles and both blenders up to the rooftop terrace.

By 7:30, we were all gathered on the roof. Max and Roger were handling the drinks while Maggie, Janet and I put together a frozen treat fixing bar. The oversized sink up there was the perfect space to encase the frozen drinks in ice. Especially, since the freezer was packed full of about 20 different pints of ice cream. Seeing it all coming together gave me such a feeling of nostalgia and joy. I stepped up behind Max as he was preparing some drinks and stood on tiptoe to whisper in his ear, "You have been such a good boy tonight that I've decided, after everyone leaves, it will be your choice of anything you desire. And, I do mean anything!" I then nibbled his earlobe, causing him to sweep me into his arms and say, "Absolutely anything?" I giggled and nodded in affirmation. He turned and whispered, "How long is everyone staying?" I swatted his behind as I walked back to complete my tasks at the fixing bar.

Max received a call from the security desk in the lobby that Mark Winslow was there a little late. Roger went down with Maggie on his arm to let Mark upstairs. Roger and Maggie were inseparable most of the night, slurping frozen treats and dancing barefoot to the music Max turned up on the speakers. Mark and Janet were more subdued, just talking as they enjoyed a different type of evening. By about 11:30, we had consumed several pizzas that Max ordered and were all feeling no pain.

Max took me by the hand and led me back downstairs and into the en suite, declaring, "They can find a bedroom or let themselves out. You're mine until sunrise!" Locking the bathroom door, Max pulled several toys from a drawer. I gasped in surprise asking where did they come from? Filling the tub with bubbles and laying out several vibrating or suction toys, he smiled that wicked smile as his eyes darkened with desire. I reached into the drawer to see what there was when he wrapped a blindfold around my head, obscuring all light from my vision. Giggling at his bravado, I used my hands to feel my way around the bathroom, pausing at his torso to feel his level of excitement.

Lifting me into the tub, I sank into the heat of the water with a moan. Suddenly, there was one of his toys vibrating its way around my breasts and between my legs. I opened, giving him total access as he purred, "Good girl." Before I could understand what was happening, Max had a butt plug inserted, and the small suctioning attachment was causing my clit to swell. It was such an overwhelming sensation while blindfolded, but I purred and gyrated like a cat, experiencing pure bliss. I must have screamed out as I went over the edge, causing Max to put his mouth on mine to silence me. We laughed as I said, "I don't care who hears. Let them all know I am experiencing Nirvana in here!" He then climbed in behind me and placed me on his lap, where I rode him reverse cowgirl until he found his release.

Removing all of the toys from the tub, Max just stroked my body with a warm cloth in the water as I melted into his heat. He whispered, "Feeling good?" eliciting my response of "So good, I don't think I'll ever move again." Just as I felt like drifting off, we heard voices calling, "We're heading out! Don't drown in there; you love birds!" Max kissed my neck and called back, "We'll catch up tomorrow?" To which Roger laughed saying it is already tomorrow! Who knew how long we had been in here exchanging the cooling water for hot again.

Max lifted me from the tub, wrapped us both in towels and walked to the bed. Before I knew it, I was sound asleep with my ear pressed to Max's chest, listening to the heartbeat that now grounded me.

When we woke later in the day, we dressed and went to my townhouse to see how far the security people had progressed. As we turned onto my street, I saw the sky explode with sparks lighting the heavens and smoke billowing, blackening the sky. The car shook with the concussive sound! Stunned, we slammed on the brakes and threw the car in reverse. I was hysterically screaming, watching my home go up in smoke, trying to open the door to jump out. Max grabbed my wrist and pulled me toward him as terror filled his expression. His phone was to his ear as he floored it out of my neighborhood. Lionel would have agents swarming in no time. But Max refused to wait to see what was going on. His only thought was to get back to the security of the penthouse, fast!

Double parking at the entrance to his building, he cut the engine and dragged me with him to the safety of the elevators. There were greetings being offered, "Good afternoon Mr. Corleone," without any response. It was transpicuous that Max was on a mission to secure us upstairs as quickly as possible. He tossed his car keys to Danny at the security desk and said, "Park my car for me please. I'll explain later." Danny gave Max a two-finger salute as the elevator doors closed. Max wrapped me in his arms as we both shook from the terrifying experience. Once inside, Max alarmed his full system and called out to me, "I need a stiff drink. You?"

With tears streaming down my face, I nodded yes. I was still trying to contain my frisson of what we saw and felt. My skin was clammy and chilled with the sense of terror I experienced while watching my life go up in smoke!

We sat on the sofa, dazed, for an undetermined amount of time before the phone began buzzing. I listened to Max's side of the conversation, knowing what was being asked "No, we didn't see anything but the explosion and flames shooting into the sky. We never left the car, I floored it into reverse and flew back to the security of the penthouse. No, I don't know if anyone was working there at the time." Then Max questioned, "Is this really necessary right now?" "Yes, We'll be here all night. Right. See you later, then."

Looking up at Max with red-rimmed eyes and such a desolate expression, I softly asked, "Would my father really try to blow me up? To kill me?" As the thoughts hit home, I lowered my head into my hands, resting them on my knees and sobbed uncontrollably. As Max reached over to pull me onto his lap, I just shook my head and jumped up, running into the bathroom and locking the door. He gave me a minute to collect myself and then followed my path to the en suite. Knocking softly, he called for me to open the door. After a minute, pounding a bit harder with no response. Max bellowed, "Baby you're scaring me! Please open the door!" Giving me another minute, he then threatened to break the door down if I didn't let him in. The lock clicked, and the door opened slowly. Looking at Max, I slid down the wall to the floor, landing with a thud. Max picked me up like a limp dishrag and carried me to the bed. But, instead of lying on the bed, we both sank to the floor. Wrapping myself around Max, I kept muttering how sorry I was.

He was trying to make me understand that this was not my doing and that nothing would make him love me any less. I looked up from under wet, spiky lashes and questioned, "How can you love me?" He responded with, "How can I not?"

We rested with our backs against the bed, rocking in each other's arms until the phone buzzed in the other room. Max was reluctant to let me go in order to answer the phone, but I pushed him away and said, "Find out what's going on, please."

Escorting Lionel and an entourage of blue-jacketed FBI people up to the penthouse was not how I wanted to spend the rest of the afternoon. Marissa had fallen asleep curled up on the bedroom floor when I went downstairs. I lifted her into the bed and tucked the covers around her, closing the light-blocking curtains and the doors. Walking back to the living room to be questioned was inevitable. I poured myself another scotch, offering a drink to anyone else. They all chimed in that they were on the clock. Falling into a chair as the adrenaline crash hit me, I was aware of five sets of eyes taking in my disheveled appearance and the dark circles under my eyes. Lionel asked, "Are you alright?" To which I responded, "Fuck No! I'm not alright, and she is even less alright!" Realizing how I sounded, I apologized.

After going over and over what we saw for well past an hour, the whole group rose to leave. I again apologized and guaranteed my call if we remembered anything else. As they left, I rearmed my security system and gave Roger a quick call. He answered with an upbeat, "Well, are you finished with all the ice cream yet?" I went dead silent, and he asked, "Max, are you still there?" Then it struck me, I had to inquire, "Were your crews done at Marissa's townhouse?" He chuckled, saying, "Hell yeah, two days ago." I muttered, "Oh thank God!" He asked why, and I told him I would call him tomorrow and hung up.

It was transpicuous that Marissa and I needed to regroup after the day's trauma. I slipped off my clothes and climbed into the bed with her. My neoteric thought as I drifted off was having her move in here permanently.

Chapter 15

Bringing the phone to my ear and speaking at a susurrus level, I answered the phone again, seeing it was Roger. Extricating myself from the bed without disturbing Marissa was difficult. She turned to her side away from me and muttered something under her breath as she again succumbed to sleep.

As I put the phone back to my ear, Roger bellowed, "What the hell Max?" "When you called earlier you couldn't enlighten me?" Max grumbled his response of needing some time to process it all. Roger then told him to allow him up since he was already in the lobby. Max's response was consent, of course. Throwing on some pants and a t-shirt, he greeted Roger with a warm slap on the back and a glass of scotch.

Closing the office door, they both planted themselves in the chairs. Max felt the need to obnubilate the office lights to suit his current demeanor. Roger told him to start from the beginning. The bruit on the street was that it was an electrical fault that ignited a gas leak in the house. Not believing that, after all that has transpired lately, Max just guffawed. Roger agreed that if this had been a peripeteia, he would agree with the word on the street. But, being another event involving Marissa's back story, it was definitely suspect. Max then thought to ask if there was any report on vicinal houses. Roger just shrugged.

Hearing the deep voices in the other room, Marissa struggled with the idea of getting up or just cocooning further into the softness of the bed. Decision made, she threw on a robe and padded barefoot down the hall. Softly knocking on the office door, she hoped she wasn't disturbing a business meeting of some sort. Roger jumped up to open the door and immediately wrapped Marissa in a tight embrace, voicing his dismay at her loss. Her eyes filled, but she blinked, containing the tears while thanking him for his consideration. He offered any service within his realm to her and also expressed the hope she would remain safe here with Max. Without thinking, she responded, "Where else would I be?" clearly delighting Max.

After recounting what they had experienced yet again, Marissa said she was famished. Roger said that he would go pick up anything they would want to eat. Running through her mental restaurant choices, Marissa said, "Italian?" Max asked if she would want to dress and go out to his cousin's restaurant or order in. She smiled and declared, "We can't hide in here forever! I want to dress and venture out if you think it's safe." Max picked up his phone to contact Fiorinos. With the promise of concealment in the back room, they donned their clothes and agreed to meet there.

Max showered quickly and shaved while Marissa primped. Entering the closet, he stopped short. Marissa turned to him wearing a deep plunging back dress in a shade of emerald green that set off her eyes and rutilant auburn tresses. The front of the dress draped loosely across her breasts but skimmed the rest of her curves. Max came up and bent to kiss the base of her spine that was exposed by the plunging fabric. Working his way up her spine, he wrapped her hair in his fist and pulled her head to the side as he sucked on her neck, eliciting a purring sound in her throat and goose flesh up her arms. She smiled and groaned, "Food or play?" He laughed and muttered, "Don't tempt me!" She reached down and grabbed a pair of Jimmy Choo stilettos and an envelope bag that she stuffed with her phone, lipstick, tissues and a credit card. He chuckled and asked, "Do you really think you need a credit card when we go out?" Her response took him by surprise when she declared, "A girl should always be prepared for anything. This little piece of plastic is for my security!" He then took her lips as he wrapped her in his arms and smiled as he said, "Now you need to fix your lipstick."

Arriving at the restaurant a few minutes late had Roger pacing out front. When Max opened Marissa's door and helped her out, Roger declared, "Now I understand your tardiness." Marissa immediately took offense, asserting her punctuality was an important personality trait to her. Laughing, he declared her attire was what caused him to comment. He could see why it would be difficult for Max to be prompt with her wearing that dress! She then relented and blew a kiss at Roger as she grasped Max's hand. Once inside the doors, Max and Roger side-eyed each other, smiling as every male head pivoted her way as she walked past. Sergio was the first to greet them and direct them to the back room. He spun to greet Max after guiding Marissa to her seat. Sergio's eyes were still on Marissa's back as he spoke to Max. Max chuckled and pointed to his eyes, saying, "I'm right up here" causing Roger to chuckle. Sergio's response was, "Donna piu bella" Max acted as dragoman, translating: "Most beautiful woman!"

The three enjoyed a complimentary Chianti from Sergio as they ordered Calamari, Caprese Salad and Crostini. The evening was a most relaxing dining experience and the conversation was light and helped to put everyone in a better mindset. By the time the second course arrived, the three had already consumed two bottles of wine. Marissa excused herself to visit the ladies' room. Entering the main dining room, all eyes were again on her. As she entered the ladies' room, she was apprehensive being the only one in there, so she locked the exterior door. While washing her hands, there was a pounding on the door. Max had evidently realized that she was alone in the open dining area. He called from the opposite side of the door, letting her know it was him. Opening the door a crack, he realized she had her stiletto off her foot, prepared to utilize it as a weapon. He grabbed her, pulling her to his chest, apologizing for not thinking clearly that she was alone out there. She laughed and said she just needed to put her shoe back on. An older gentleman strolled by and remarked to Max that she was the most beautiful creature he had ever seen! Max smiled and thanked him. Walking back to the private dining area, he kept his hand on her lower back, staking his claim for all to see.

Feeling a bit uneasy again, the three savored their meals of Veal piccata, Shrimp Risotto and Tuscan Gnocchi. They each enjoyed an espresso after the meal, but decided to forego dessert. Sergio came out and sat with them for a few minutes hearing about the harrowing experiences lately. He regarded Max and his lady and offered any resources his Italian "family" could supply. Max laughed, stating he would rather not bring "Family" into anything related to him, but thanks for the offer. Marissa regarded Max with raised eyebrows and a smirk. He just shrugged.

Leaving the restaurant with full stomachs and a rejuvenated spirit, they all sauntered to the vehicles in the lot. Roger was the first to see someone lurking in the shadows and practically pushed Marissa into the car. Max jumped in the driver's side and was on the road in just a few seconds. Flooring the engine, they were propelled from the lot like a rock from a slingshot. He jostled Marissa as if she were the ball in a pinball machine, weaving in and out, passing multiple cars in succession. She glanced over at his face of pure concentration as he maneuvered through D.C. traffic. His phone was buzzing in his pocket during the entire ride.

Relaxing, once they exited the car in the underground parking garage, Max pulled his phone out to check it. Seeing the message on the screen caused Max to laugh, drawing Marissa's attention. Roger wanted them to know he confronted the man in the shadows at the restaurant once they left. It was a man Lionel had following them for security. Max waited until he and Marissa were inside the penthouse before he phoned Lionel to ream him out! "A heads up would have made sense if you were going to have security on our tails! I could have killed us escaping that lot at break-neck speed!" Lionel chuckled and said, "Slow down there ace. This was done at the last minute when we saw you leave the building. Would you have even answered my call at the restaurant?" Max stopped his tirade, realizing they must have been watching them all day. Asking Lionel, "We now have a security detail?" Lionel chuckled again, stating, "And God knows you need it with your lady on your arm. It's not like she doesn't draw all kinds of attention!" Max smiled and muttered, "That she does."

Plans were made for Lionel and a few of the agents to meet at Max's penthouse in the morning. Max and Marissa would then be introduced to the men and women who would be observing their lives from a discrete distance. Questions would be answered then, also, about what was discovered at Marissa's townhouse. Anything that was salvageable would be boxed and brought up to them at that point.

As a final topping on their evening, Max suggested some plain old vanilla sex as dessert. Grinning, Marissa admonished him, stating "You or I wouldn't even know how to do that!" He helped her undress and offered her a boring culmination to their evening. Chuckling, she granted him full access and control over the remainder of their evening. Groaning, he remarked, "Who's idea was vanilla anyway?"

Throwing her naked body over his shoulder, he stomped from the closet. Tossing her on the bed and watching her bounce once before he pounced gave him the incentive to get creative. Crawling up over her, he stood straddling her on the bed and smirked down at her. She giggled and suggested that she would be wrapped around him in no time if he would submit. "What is vanilla about that idea?" he asked as a thought struck him. Bounding from the room, he yelled over his shoulder, "Don't move!" Moments later, he came in holding a pint of plain vanilla ice cream and a serving spoon, causing her to giggle even more. "So this is your idea of vanilla sex?" His response was just a growl.

Hours later, in the shower, they scrubbed sticky ice cream from all kinds of crevices and orifices. Laughing, she remarked that vanilla sex was kind of sweet and filling but extremely sticky! And now, they needed to change the sheets! He licked her neck, causing her to shiver, explaining that he missed a spot! And they laughed in unison. He suddenly declared, "I love you, Marissa!" She turned around sweetly, smiling her affirmation, "And, I you!" Turning off the water, he picked her up and carried her back to bed.

Chapter 16

Lionel and a half dozen agents filed into the lobby the next morning. Mark and Roger weren't far behind. They descended to the garage, checking security there, and then circumvented the entire lobby area, opened and enclosed spaces. Roger texted Max to let him know they were on their way up, when the elevator doors opened and Max strode out.

The weather outside was turning cooler, prompting Max to don a cashmere sweater over his jeans. Roger snickered at his need to always present himself as a complete package. In contrast, Roger was wearing his weekend at-home attire of sweats and joggers. Mark took both men in, smiling at the contrast between the best friends. Waiting for the food to arrive that he had ordered was what prompted Max to come to the lobby. Just then, a catering truck pulled up out front and unloaded two carts of provisions and a chef and two-person wait staff. Max took them up first, instructing Roger to escort the entourage up in the next elevator.

The caterer had everything set up in no time. There would now be a hot breakfast for everyone. Max planned to have them sit around the dining table, which had the capacity to seat 16 comfortably. Marissa came sauntering down the hall just as everyone was entering the foyer. She was wearing a skin-tight pair of charcoal gray jeans with a gray leopard print silk blouse that was sheer enough to see every detail of her soft gray Lace camisole underneath. She wore her signature stilettos in deep crimson, matching her wide waist-defining Crimson belt. Her hair was done in soft curls over her shoulders, held with a clip above her ear on the right side. As always, no one missed her entry. Lionel whistled as Max went over to kiss her. Lionel's comment was heard even though he was just murmuring his thoughts out loud. "Does she ever look undone like the rest of mankind?" Marissa heard and laughed, saying, "I hope I'm never that complacent!" All of the people behind Lionel snickered at him getting caught.

Max directed everyone to the table as the chef brought out the first portion of their meal. He presented a borek of filo dough filled with savory goose and stilton cheese, a spinach and bacon quiche, apple and fresh squeezed orange juice, and multiple carafes of a selection of teas or coffees, all labeled. He announced, "The eggs benedict and chocolate waffles would be out shortly, but save room for the Tarte aux Fraises and the jumbo sugared blueberries with zabaglione sauce." Everyone's eyes lit up with his menu! One of the agents commented that this was a first and new experience, saying, "And we all hope you will feel our gratitude for such extravagance." Max smiled and said, "Thank you all for watching over us!"

After everyone was filled into a state of food coma, the table was cleared. Lionel suggested they go over the events that had instigated the show of force in the room. He explained that the explosion of the townhouse was set using an incendiary device on each of the 3 floors and then opening an incoming gas line. There was very little salvageable. He placed a small box in front of Marissa, explaining that her fireproof lock box was the only thing not damaged beyond recognition. Marissa breathed a sigh of relief, disclosing that the box held everything she had left from her mother. Lionel then asked each of the agents to introduce themselves and reveal what they had found during the intense investigation so far.

The first agent on the table then introduced himself as Jack Riser and detailed his computer hacking skills used to trace Malcolm Calloway's online presence. Next was Terry Murphy, who revealed his deep dive into Marissa's father's finances. Tommy Halverson stated, in one word, that his job was "Security." Next, Brian O'Connor revealed his phone tapping and tracing of Mr. Calloway. Next was Jennifer Reed, who was to be Marissa's shadow until Mr. Calloway was apprehended. And lastly, David Martin, who would also be security. His presence would be seen in the lobby at all times unless redirected by Lionel. Lionel told Marissa that she was to go nowhere outside of this penthouse without Jennifer at her side! Max voiced his thanks for their vigilance.

As the agents rose to leave, Lionel told each one their shifts and directives would be noted on their phones by the time they returned to headquarters. They all shook Max and Marissa's hands and thanked them for their thoughtfulness and generosity. Jennifer then gave Marissa her card, pointing out that her cell as well as direct line at the agency were listed. She reiterated the directive that Marissa call her at whatever time of the day or night she is needed. She explained that until this assignment is over, she will be on the 7th floor, where the FBI has rented a small apartment for her, so she is accessible anytime, day or night. She then handed Max one also, letting him know that he could call anytime he would need to have security for Marissa, for any reason. Marissa should not be alone at any time until this case is wrapped up. He then promised to add Jennifer to the biometrics for access to the elevators and to arm or disarm the security system in an emergency.

Once they were gone, Max, Marissa, Roger and Mark sat with Lionel for full disclosure. Lionel expressed concern for Marissa in particular. He disclosed what had so far been uncovered. It appeared that Malcolm Calloway, the 3rd, had joined a foreign black market group in the past 8 years, who now had him by the balls. He was up to his eyebrows in financial involvement with the contacts from Minsk and Bucharest. Part of their business was the sex trafficking of young women. Marissa's hand flew up to her mouth as she gasped. "How? Why?" were all she seemed to be able to utter. Lionel nodded and said that he understood her shock, but there was more. Her father was laundering money for this organization initially. He was using art transfer and sales through two of his shell companies to cover these activities. But more importantly, Interpol was following his involvement in weapons trading. Max then asked, "But how is this tied to the events surrounding Marissa's and even my abduction?"

As Lionel laid all of the information they had already collected on the table, Max watched all of the color leave Marissa's face, and her eyes become glassy. He asked if she was alright just as she slumped in her chair. Grabbing her and lifting her into his arms, he carried her to the sofa. He yelled for Roger to pour her a brandy. Max placed her with her feet elevated on the arm and her head flat to bring the blood back to her head. As she opened her eyes, she apologized for her emotional reaction. Roger had her sip some of the brandy to help rejuvenate her. Once she was feeling better, Max suggested they gather in the living room so she could remain lying down with her head in Max's lap. She was insistent that she sit up to hear the remainder of the report. So, Max sat with his arm around her shoulder, her leaning into him, more for his sake than hers.

Lionel continued to divulge that, evidently, this particular group found that Marissa, Malcolm's daughter, would be a good bargaining chip with her father to keep him invested in their activities. "That is part of why Mr.

Calloway bequeathed the villa and all of its contents to Marissa. By doing so, he put more emphasis on her wealth and decreased his. Little did he know that she would become a target of a much more refined machine than his little game with the gallery and Jonathan Abrams. This whole thing started as a game of control between Mr. Calloway and his daughter. It has now morphed into a much more dangerous position for Marissa to be in. These international groups are much more dangerous. The only positive is that Interpol is closing in on the group and has already shut down several ventures. But, until the head of the snake has been removed, Marissa is in danger."

It was then suggested that Marissa and now, by association, Max be vigilant and remain in this secure location for an extended period of time. Marissa then asked the question on the tip of everyone's tongues "How long exactly do you think this will take?" Lionel then looked at his shoes and murmured, "Maybe up to a year." Marissa screeched, "A YEAR?" He blanched and said hopefully not that long, but we can't be sure how effectively this whole thing can be shut down. Max then questioned about possibly traveling somewhere for a break. Lionel said that would not be wise unless they did it with a security force traveling on a private jet. Max smiled and looked at Marissa, saying, "We can do that when you need some time away." She responded with, "That's so expensive!" Roger then laughed, stating,

"You know who you are saying that to, right?!?" Max shot him a scathing look, and everyone laughed.

After getting past the logistics of life as a prisoner of circumstance, The mood in the room lightened. Max turned to Mark and asked what kind of security he would have access to. Roger looked over Mark's head and suggested, "Talk to your cousin Sergio Fiorino about his contacts." Max blushed, saying he would rather not involve that portion of his family, using air quotes again, emphasizing "FAMILY". Mark then responded with, "Oh I get it now!" He then went on to suggest a security company that some friends put together with retired special ops and navy seal persons. Lionel spoke up, saying, "That would be perfect. They would understand the threat better than most.

Marissa was beginning to feel like she was at a tennis match, with her head going side to side as each man suggested something else. She then got up and excused herself. Going to the bedroom, she grabbed her phone and gave her best friend Maggie a call. She just needed to get away from all of the anxiety-provoking logistics for a while. She needed some "girl talk and girl time."

Chapter 17

After seeing the men leave the condo, Max went back into the bedroom, only to find Marissa lying on the bed naked and spread out on the bed in an "X". Her arms and legs were spread as wide as she could place them, holding onto the headboard. A mischievous smile on her face told Max everything he needed to know. Marissa motioned to the chocolate syrup and the whipped cream, smiling, and in a sultry voice, said, "Care for some dessert after such dark conversations?" He smiled and pulled his sweater over his head, dropping it to the floor as he unbuttoned his jeans. She maintained her spread-out position as she hit the remote, turning down the lights. "I've been waiting patiently for you, big boy, so there better be some enthusiasm!" He laughed and said, "You are so good when you are bad," bringing a coy smile to her face.

Marissa reached over and sprayed the whipped cream on his groin and exclaimed, "That's what I have been waiting for!" As Max climbed over her, she held his manhood with both of her hands. She was salivating already and couldn't wait any longer. She took all of him into her mouth with a moan. Working him to the point of no return, he withdrew from her mouth. He then drizzled chocolate onto some of his favorite spots on her curvaceous body. Max dribbled the chocolate, Starting from her neck and then going onto her inner biceps, underarms, breasts, and the inner part of her opened thighs. Then, while looking into her eyes, he licked all the chocolate off her, tasting and smelling Marissa's naked body, which was now sweaty and writhing in absolute ecstasy. Marissa let out a loud, sultry moan, as they both enjoyed their desserts with a plethora of sounds from each. "I can't wait any longer Max! I want all of you right now. I want it hard and fast!"

Max, being the tease that he was, licked his way up her torso gently and slowly as Marissa purred and writhed with pleasure under him. He then wasted no time in diving deep within her heat as she urged him on, asking for him to put everything into her, causing a violent release. They both made their ecstasy known simultaneously with screams of passion. She told him, "Tonight's gonna be a night for continuous passion, only if you can handle it, big boy!" She felt insatiable! Max slid down her body to satisfy her desires with his mouth. She wove her fingers through his hair, holding him where she wanted him until she couldn't stand any more stimulation. She questioned his readiness when he rose, displaying his desire for her yet again. The night continued on like that for hours before they collapsed in each other's arms.

Waking to the sound of both his and her phone gave them pause. Looking at each other with confusion, Max answered his phone first. The security desk was alerting him to the arrival of a package at the desk. He told them he was not expecting anything and deferred to the FBI agent who was supposed to be in the lobby. After a few moments holding the phone to his ear, the line went dead. Marissa then checked her phone message. It was Janet from the gallery declaring the gallery had been broken into overnight. The police were currently there and wanted to speak with her.

Feeling the hairs on his neck bristle, Max grabbed Marissa and directed her to call Lionel and have him send people over immediately. Dressing hastily, Marissa was on the brink of tears; not knowing how to handle this situation was discomfiting. Max then placed a call to Mark, describing what had transpired. Mark told him to stay put and not leave the penthouse. That was the fortress that was needed to protect them with all of the confusing activities going on. Max and Marissa went to the kitchen for coffee while waiting for Lionel to arrive with backup. The main thought in the back of Max's mind was, *Where is Tommy Halverson???* The security person who was supposed to be stationed in the lobby wasn't there.

As the FBI swarmed the lobby along with the police in full tactical gear, Lionel let Max know they were in the building. He advised Max to keep Marissa in the penthouse until they had cleared the garage and lobby. Max grabbed onto Marissa and marched her to the sofa. He then explained that Tommy was missing, but, while he was doing that, Lionel had agents going over the building. Shaking uncontrollably, Marissa questioned if they should have Jennifer brought up from the 7th floor with her sidearm. Max unlocked a concealed cabinet beneath the kitchen island and retrieved his "Glock 18" declaring to have the ability to protect them if needed. Marissa claimed to feel better about that but showed no signs of relaxing.

Waiting for some word was excruciating. Just sitting on the sofa with hundreds of scenarios playing out in their minds was almost panic-inducing!

When Max's phone rang in his hand, they were both startled! Answering before the second ring, Max bellowed, "What is happening?" Lionel alerted them that Tommy was found, but was now being transported to the hospital for observation after being tested for a concussion by the EMT. He reported that someone was seen trying to break into the locked door leading to the garage. Tommy followed him, and he was jumped as soon as the doors opened. He was immediately immobilized by a substantial hit to his head. We found him next to your car, Max! This was obviously a message for us. Max then inquired how he was jumped in the supposedly secure garage? It was reported that they are going through all video feeds right now to determine the who and how. He told Max to sit tight for a few more minutes, and he will hopefully have some answers.

Max filled large mugs with freshly brewed coffee while they waited. He put on music and put his hand out to Marissa with a smile. She stared at his hand for a moment before inquiring, "What?" He told her to take his hand, and they will be mentally transported to a better place. He pulled her into his arms and began to swirl her around the open floor space in a rhythmic pattern. As her shoulders began to relax, she closed her eyes and let the music transport her somewhere else. Max was an excellent dance partner who made her feel as though she could float as long as her hand was in his. He whispered in her ear, "We can go anywhere you want to go with the music." She giggled, "Anywhere?" He smiled and kissed her on that sensitive spot below her ear as he responded softly, "Yes."

After drifting in Max's arms for a few moments, Marissa suggested they dress while waiting instead of possibly greeting Lionel and those with him in robes with nothing underneath. Max laughed and agreed.

Marissa pulled a camel-colored cashmere sweater dress from the closet and a pair of Ferragamo boots. Max threw on his jeans and another cashmere turtleneck. Regarding each other with approval, they grabbed their phones and started for the hall. Max's phone rang again. Seeing it was Lionel, he nodded to Marissa and answered before the second ring again. Lionel asked to be allowed to speak with them upstairs in person.

Max greeted Lionel, Jennifer, David and a new pair of agents for the lobby. Sitting in the living room, Lionel introduced Abe Kaufmann and Tim Donelly. Both men looked as if they were WWE fighters. Both were built like brick walls, well over 6'6" tall. When they shook hands with Marissa, her hand disappeared in theirs. Lionel explained that these both were former Special Ops members and were often used as personal security when needed. Marissa inquired about Jennifer still being her person. Lionel laughed and explained that in spite of her 5'6" height and slim build, she is trained in all manor of martial arts and was top of her class at Quantico. Tim Donelly spoke up, describing the first time he faced off with Jennifer in training. She took him down before he knew what hit him. He chuckled and reported, "That will never happen again." He claimed to believe he had to not go full force since she was female, stating he now knows not to ever hold back and make assumptions.

The daily schedule was then explained. If Marissa wanted to go to the gallery at any time, she needed to have Jennifer with her and be driven by one of the security detail. Max would be assigned Abe for his security if he needed to go anywhere. They would be on call at any time. There would also be an Armored black SUV at their disposal, thanks to Max's generosity. Marissa shot Max a look, causing him to mutter, "Need to know you are safe," under his breath. Lionel apprised her of Max's discretionary fund set up for their security. "He spared no expense!" Marissa smiled and asked if they would be allowed to attend the club on Thursday nights. Lionel laughed, being aware of their membership. The others looked at him quizzically, causing him to report they would be made aware of the details later. Suffice it to say they now had shadows wherever they went!

Max offered to have breakfast brought in for them while they were in the penthouse. Lionel declined the offer, stating he had a lot of information to update security with. They then said their goodbyes and exchanged cell numbers and agency numbers. Of course, Lionel expressed his involvement in everything. "Call me any time it's necessary for any reason! I will still be the lead on your case until it is closed." Marissa then bent her head and muttered, "Possibly by year's end." Causing Lionel to squeeze her hand as he passed by.

Alone again in the penthouse, Max told her to call Janet at the gallery and see if she was doing OK. "Let her know that Lionel will be contacting the local police to inform them of the situation should they uncover something linking the break-in to the FBI's case." Sighing deeply, Marissa picked up her phone and dialed Janet's personal number. Explaining the whole debacle to Janet gave Marissa heart palpitations. By the time she was finished, Janet held her breath before reporting a phone call for Marissa from her father on Monday morning. Marissa asked if he had left any message. Then she told Janet she would be in to speak with her in person before Janet left the gallery this afternoon. Terminating the call, she looked up at Max and asked if they could go assess what may be missing or damaged at the gallery today. He nodded affirmatively and dialed Lionel's number. Explaining the situation to Lionel, Max was assured someone would be there to transport them and stay with them while they took care of the Gallery's business. He asked if 3:00 p.m. would work for them, getting a yes in response.

It felt like the hours leading up to 3:00 p.m. dragged on. Max and Marissa busied themselves with updating files and notes. Documenting anything they could think of that may not have been reported initially. Marissa then thought of someone she hadn't thought of since she was a small child. She has a distant cousin whom the family visited in Australia when she was 5 or 6 years old. Her name at that time was Meg Calloway. She was somewhere around 20 years old then, making Meg around 45-50 years old now. This felt like a loose thread that Marissa was able to pull. She reported this revelation to Max, who immediately called Roger. He requested that Roger have his IT person do a deep dive into the name Margaret or Meg Calloway in Australia. Feeling hopeful that Marissa just uncovered an important link to a possible place of refuge for her father, he smiled to himself.

Lionel showed up at 2:55 and called up to Max's number. Max and Marissa were sitting on pins and needles, waiting for their security detail to arrive. They picked up Jennifer on the 7th floor on their way to the lobby. Lionel and Abe were there waiting. As they entered the armored SUV, Marissa giggled about Max going over the top with the mode of transportation. Lionel slid into the Driver's seat, Jennifer climbed into the shotgun seat, and Abe slid in the back, sandwiching Marissa between him and Max.

Marissa thought Max was built, but Abe was like a freight train. His thighs were triple the size of hers, and his arms were rock solid against her side. And she couldn't deny the heat his body emanated. He definitely offered a sense of security if his build had any bearing on it.

When they pulled up to the gallery, there was a blue and white district police car there waiting for them. Lionel spoke over his shoulder, reporting he called ahead. Marissa, Max, Jennifer and Abe entered the gallery, startling the three customers perusing the art selections. Janet ushered them into the back in order to show Marissa the Matisse that was ruined with red spray paint and a small local artist's works slashed and knocked to the floor, damaging the frames. Janet reported that the files had been rummaged through and were strewn all over the office. She didn't know if anything was missing from Marissa's private files she never went into.

Marissa immediately went to her personal files with trepidation. She had a feeling the files with her father's contacts would be missing. Janet had just stacked all of the files behind the desk. Pulling a box from the shelf, Marissa began piling everything from the floor into it to go through from home. Janet told her the insurance company had already sent an adjuster over to photograph the damage. After filling two file boxes with paper and taking some file folders with her, Marissa said she had seen enough.

Driving back to the penthouse, Marissa explained the need to go through her files to see if this was indeed linked to their case. Lionel then apprised them of the report filed with the district police. Both she and Max were satisfied with the current state of affairs and just wanted to unwind in peace and quiet for a while.

Max addressed his thoughts with Marissa once they were ensconced in the safety of the home. He said he would like to plan a trip somewhere warm and sunny for a few days when Marissa felt able to get away. He inquired if she had ever been to Belize. Going somewhere like that with white sandy beaches where their security could follow seemed feasible. She threw her arms around his neck and kissed him passionately in a response. He took it a step further, lifting her into his arms and wrapping her legs around his waist as he carried her to the back bedroom.

Max had her clothes off in no time, and his sweater was on the floor with his jeans undone. Marissa was naked by the time he toed off his shoes and dropped his jeans along with his boxers at the foot of the bed. He put his finger up as a sign for her to wait a minute and hustled into the closet. Exiting with a crop and some massage oils, he expressed his anticipation of their games. She had that look in her eyes that he always was aroused by. Coming to the bed, he placed his toys on the side table and climbed up her body, trapping her beneath him for a deep kiss that extended to a full-body exploration!

The crop was then brought over to tease those nipples and vulva. Once Max had her moaning and writhing, he turned to do a massage with heated oil. She grabbed him by the balls and began her own massage. By the time they were both satisfied with the stimulation, Max threw her legs over his shoulders again. Kneeling between her legs, he lifted her bottom off of the bed and found the perfect angle for both of them. Increasing the pace, she pushed him off her and reached into the concealed drawer under the bed to retrieve the nipple clamps and cock ring to add to their enjoyment. He moaned as she attached the ring and couldn't wait to begin again, knowing how the ring extended his orgasm and how the clamps affected hers. It wasn't until they both found their release that they opened their eyes, panting and sweating. He dropped her legs to the bed and collapsed next to her, smiling. "I don't think I will ever get bored of playing with you. You are so responsive!"

The following morning there was a call from the security desk that there was a delivery. Max threw on his sweats and a t-shirt and went down to grant their entrance to the penthouse. When the elevator doors opened, Tim Donelly was speaking to the purported delivery person. Max smiled and informed him that, this time, it was an expected delivery. Abe then stood and informed Max that they would accompany the delivery man to the unit and then escort him out when done.

Chapter 18

The delivery person not only delivered but assembled the apparatus for Max in his gym. Both Abe and Tim asked how it was used since they had never seen that particular gym apparatus before. Marissa, wrapped in a fuzzy robe and barefoot, giggled at the door, waiting for Max's description. He blew her a kiss and asked if she wanted to demonstrate how it was used. She threw the paperback book from her hand at him and replied, "You're on your own this time, lover", chuckling the entire way back to the bedroom. When she reached the bedroom door, she yelled over her shoulder, "Thank you!"

Max then enlightened the two muscle men about the use of the device as the delivery guy snickered. Abe's eyes were like saucers as Tim repeated, "Saint Andrews Cross, huh?" And what other "toys" do you use? Max smiled and asked them if they were to accompany them to the club Thursday night. They both answered "Affirmative". Max winked and said maybe you can tour the Red Room before it's used on Marissa's reserved time. They explained that they would be required to clear any room that Max and Marissa would go into. Smiling and clearing their throats, they agreed to escort the delivery person out.

Thursday night afforded Marissa joyous anticipation of the evening outside of the condo. Max was finishing in the shower as she dried her hair and applied her makeup. She inquired if Max had a preference for what she should wear tonight. He grabbed her ass and groaned nothing! She chuckled and said that might be a bit chilly, to which he replied, "I promise to warm you up baby." "Ok then you get no input. I'll surprise you," she replied.

Max was dressed in his favorite Italian silk suit, waiting in the living room, fixing a drink at the bar. When she drifted into the room, she was wearing a copper suede mid-length dress with a slit to her hip and long sleeves with a high fitted neckline. As she spun for him, all he could see was skin to the base of her spine. The dress was backless except for the gold lariat chain that fell down her spine in the open back of the dress, touching the dimpled indentations at her buttocks when she moved. The copper suede could have been spray painted on, giving the hint of no undergarments to cause lines of any sort. She wore her favorite stilettos, this time in gold, and grabbed a small gold beaded bag that fit in her palm. The only jewelry besides the lariat were the gold hoops adorning her ears. He told her she always took his breath away!

He approached her, placing his drink on the end table and ran his hand up her exposed leg to the top. "I thought so," he moaned. She smiled and explained that the suede was unforgiving and anything under it would detract from the line. He grabbed her camel merino wool wrap coat and tied it tightly around her, saying "I'm the only one who gets to look at that nakedness under there." She grabbed onto his arm and said, "Without any argument from me! Shall we?"

When the elevator doors opened, Tim and Abe were suited to perfection and ready to accompany them to the club. Arriving at precisely 9:30, Marissa blew a kiss to Bart at the door and motioned that the guys were with her. Bart smiled and informed her, "We all got that word, Flame." Abe and Tim looked at Max and questioned, "Flame?" Max chuckled and said he forgot to let them know, "That was the only name she was known by here."

Once inside, Max took her coat from her and handed it to the coat check girl, who sent a flirty smile to the bodyguards. They were busy ogling "Flame" dress and the club itself when they noticed that every head in the room turned to take in "Flame." Watching her hips swing as she strolled to the bar, they were mesmerized. When she put her foot on the bar footrest as she reached for her drink that Gary had already placed on the napkin for her, Abe choked out loud as Tim murmured, "Holy Shit" under his breath as he gawked at Max. Max laughed and softly commented, "I don't understand my luck, that's for sure." She told Gary to give the guys anything they wanted and blew him a kiss. He motioned, slapping his cheek as if he caught it and said, "Anything for you gorgeous".

Max directed them toward the Red Room, past the observation window. Abe blushed as they walked past, seeing the threesome enjoying the voyeurs and watching them pleasure each other. Tim put his head down and kept walking. Flame then opened the door with her keycard so the guys could make certain the space was cleared for them. Max showed them the different "Toys" to be enjoyed and opened the cabinet displaying the extensive collection of Shibari silk ropes, swings, harnesses, whips, floggers, crops, handcuffs, nipple clamps, various c-rings and vibration and suction devices. Abe was wandering around the room checking out the poles and crosses and bondage apparatus when Tim commented "I think we are living a boring life!" Marissa chuckled and said, "There is always room for titillation and extreme pleasure, no matter how vanilla you believe your sex life to be!" Abe looked up and said, "Non-existent?" They all laughed. Max asked if they were cleared to use the room now.

Abe and Tim left with the reassurance that one would be posted by the door and the other would be meandering around, watching for anything concerning. Marissa reminded them that they had an open bar tab, which included food if they wanted. Abe commented that he didn't think he could eat here after the tour. He was too worked up and didn't want any distractions.

"Flame" closed and locked the door as they left and found Max kneeling in front of her, pushing the slit open on her dress and placing his mouth where he knew he would get to her. She leaned against the door and moaned as he kissed up her inner thighs, placing her left leg over his shoulder and running his tongue over her until she quivered. He then stood and walked to the cabinet. She sauntered over as she dropped the suede dress to the floor, baring herself completely. She then stood behind him and ran her hands up and down his hardness, cupping his balls and making him moan as she unzipped and pushed his pants down his legs.

He chose the Shibari ropes this time with the harness to suspend her from the ceiling over the bed. She chose the feather tickler and magic vibrating wand for anal stimulation causing Max's eyes to darken with lust. "Every time is different and sexually stimulating with you my love," she whispered in his ear. He just growled and began wrapping her in the ropes. Once she was suspended above the bed with the harness, he lowered her onto his erection, leaving her hands free to utilize the anal vibrator. They were both past the point of stimulation when Max lowered her all the way down, causing his most intense orgasm after she experienced her three. She laid next to him, after being untied, and ran the tickler up and down his body. He remarked that he didn't think he could go again that quickly, but his body was responding immediately to the sensations. He leaned over her, circling her clit with his thumb until she couldn't take any more stimulation. She climbed on for a reverse cowgirl ride and took them over the edge within seconds. Panting, he grabbed her around the waist and licked and suckled her neck and breasts, causing her to shiver in his arms. After resting in each other's arms for half an hour, Max asked if she was ready to get another drink and head out. He then got up and grabbed a warm, moist towel to wipe her body down before they got dressed.

Checking her reflection in the mirror, Marissa asked Max, "Do I have that freshly-fucked look?" He laughed and said, "You do most of the time!" She swatted his arm and said, "The room sure smells of sex." He smiled and declared, "We could bottle the pheromones you emit and make a fortune!" Tidying up the room a bit, they stepped out into the hall. Abe and Tim were right there. She almost tripped on them exiting the room. Laughing, she asked if they could have a drink with them now that their night was almost over. They responded with, "Not until you are both safely tucked away in your fortress." She looked back to Max, who said, "Let's head home then, and you can enjoy a nightcap with us."

Seated on the sofa, Max and Marissa were wrapped in each other's embrace, her legs crossed, only revealing the left exposed leg to the hip. Max was feeding her sips of bourbon. Abe was taking in the spectacular view while enjoying a scotch with Max. Tim was seated in the swivel barrel chair sipping a beer when he wondered if he could ask us something. Max and Marissa both nodded sure. Tim was curious about how we got involved in the alternative sex scene. That caught Abe's attention, who then sat down to hear the response. Marissa began with her story of boring dates and an unfulfilled sexual appetite throughout college until someone took her to a club one night just to observe. She said she thought it looked enticing and exciting to be able to orchestrate an alternate evening of pleasure. Max agreed, saying his experience was similar until he joined the Coeur Noir Club and was invited to the Red Room by this temptress by the "nom de plume" of Flame. "Seeing her auburn hair under the lights and the silk wrap dress that hinted at the underlying gift to be unwrapped, I was hooked. Even though I had already paid my entrance fee, if I didn't like it after my first week, I could withdraw. But after that first night, that was not an option!"

Both Abe and Tim laughed and said, "We can see where the temptation was great. But not everyone is dissatisfied with vanilla sex," was Tim's response. Abe chuckled and said, "Not everyone has been getting any lately." They all voiced that the degree of sexual preference is what keeps things spicy or "normal" for others. With that, Tim rose and said that their morning was going to be here before they knew it and thanked them for the drink. Abe said his goodnights and voiced his gratitude for the drink and education. Marissa blew them each a kiss and said sleep well. Going out the door, Abe commented, "I don't think I'll be able to close my eyes again without some kind of wet dream after tonight." Tim punched him in the arm and said that's what cold showers are for. Going down in the elevator, Tim asked Abe if he thought there was anything under that dress that Flame was wearing. Abe chuckled and said, "I wouldn't have minded finding out." Tim shook his head and said, "Perv!"

Exiting the elevator, the guys saw David at his post and nodded as they left the building. "This sure has been a unique assignment," was Tim's take. Abe just grunted his agreement and yawned. They both missed the man in the shadows across the street watching them. David, on the other hand, was well aware and had already alerted Lionel of the man lurking across the street. His shift was going to be exciting!

As the SUVs descended on the block from both ends, the man tried to walk away nonchalantly. However, the agents had other thoughts. He was bundled into one of the SUVs and on the way to headquarters in a matter of minutes for interrogation. Cursing himself for getting caught after feeling so smug that the other two gorillas had completely missed him.

Transport to headquarters afforded Nicholai time to develop a plausible story of why he was lurking in the shadows. He was instructed to observe the coming and going of Marissa, but if that were to include Max, so be it. Those two were inseparable over the past few weeks since their rescue from the idiot who worked at the

Calloway Gallery. Mr. Calloway was to blame for that debacle.

Those in higher places weren't pleased with how Malcolm Calloway handled things. He brought attention to things that he wasn't even aware were happening behind the scenes. Calloway's connections from Budapest now have Interpol looking into things that have run effectively until this point in time.

Nicholai believes he should not be on anyone's radar. His credentials show him as a CIA operative instead of part of a sleeper cell activated within the past month. Once he is within the FBI headquarters, he should be able to get access to his contact within that organization to vouch for his legitimacy.

The web just continues to tangle more and more people in it.

Trafficking and arms were a lucrative trade whether handled overseas or here in the States. Mr. Calloway is up to his eyebrows in both. Using art that is sold legitimately through his daughter's gallery has been part of the information train running through the states. Pieces that Marissa's gallery has been procuring for specific clients here have had information encoded in the frames or the actual artwork, depending on the medium. She has been completely unaware of her complicity in this network. The system worked well until Malcolm Calloway got his nose out of joint over his daughter's success in the art business. Trying to undermine her through lawsuits and injunctions drew Max Corleone, esquire, into the fray. Now, everyone who was not seen as participating is being watched or guarded by the FBI, temporarily shutting down the network.

Chapter 19

The tracing of Malcolm Calloway the 3rd's accounts and communications had opened up new avenues for the FBI and Interpol. The information that had been gleaned from phone traces and overseas financial tracking had disclosed more contacts and information than they had been able to uncover over the past three years between both agencies. Unfortunately, Lionel saw this as being a bigger threat to Max and Marissa than they initially thought. Breaking down some of the people apprehended had proven daunting. This last man picked up across the street from the penthouse of Max Corleone, had proven to be an unexpected can of worms. Nicholai Brezinski claimed to be CIA and had reached out to a higher-up here at the FBI, thinking he is part of a sleeper cell that had recently been activated. Unfortunately for Mr Brezinski, his FBI contact was really a double agent, if you will, loyal to the FBI. But they now had some bargaining power since he was apprehended.

They now knew that there had been coded messages within some of the art pieces that Marissa had brokered deals for clients in D.C. They knew that she was unaware of the deals because Interpol had been following them for several years, waiting to shut down the communications. All of this intrigue would be causing her business trouble as pieces that were coming in were being confiscated at the ports, and clients she had procured the pieces for were now being questioned. It was unclear how far up in D.C. society this network reached. And, of course, the farther up it went, the more at risk Marissa and Max became.

Unaware of the depth of their involvement, Max and Marissa sat in the penthouse, laptop on the bed in front of them, selecting places they would love to go. Max pointed out the tropical paradises that could be secure locations to visit while Marissa dreamt of white sand, sun and aqua waters to float in. She tantalized Max by talking about her black string bikini with the thong bottom. He finished her description with, "That no one will see but me?" She laughed and explained that he would get to see her nude after she has developed tan lines.

Rising from the bed, Max asked if Marissa would like another nightcap before they retire. Smiling that temptress smile, she whispered "Is there any more of that chocolate liqueur for me to lick off your body? I'm feeling the need for something sweet!" Max's response was to climb back on the bed and address his need for something sweet and wet as he spread her legs and crawled between them with a glint in his eyes. Giggling, Marissa admonished him with, "But I need something sweet in MY mouth!" "That can be arranged later," came the reply. Max moaned, and as his mouth found her core, she grabbed his head, running her fingers through his waves and hissed "You are insatiable!"

Nothing is more relaxing late at night than a good roll in the sheets, Max thought to himself, pulling the covers over her limp body and snuggling, with his hand still caressing her hip. He ran his thumb in concentric circles over her silky skin, wondering how long they will have to be holed up in this tower. *Not that I mind having her always by my side.* His concern was her ability to comfortably withdraw from the outside world. After losing her townhouse in the explosion, she had been docile and comfortable. *How long can that last though, with imprisonment in my "ivory tower"?* Listening to her breathing into his chest, he succumbed to sleep with these thoughts.

Waking in a cold bed startled Max awake! Glancing at his phone on the nightstand, he couldn't believe he slept until 9:45. Listening for sounds from the ensuite or kitchen, Max stretched and managed to throw his legs over the side of the bed to rise. Grabbing a pair of workout shorts and pulling them on, he made his way down the hall. Overhearing Marissa on the phone in the living room, he paused to try to discern who she was speaking with. "But, Janet, we can't lose that client! Do you realize they have been the most substantial money maker for the gallery?" Then there was a pause before she yelled, "They said WHAT? How dare they imply I caused them to be investigated and interrogated! This is outrageous! I'll be there in an hour. Let me go get dressed. I'll see you shortly."

Max entered the room, startling her. "Trouble at the gallery? I'll call Lionel for our secure transportation and go with you." Shaking her head and murmuring under her breath, she said, "You don't have to go, I can handle this on my own." Feeling dismissed, Max replied, "Suit yourself, but you WILL take security!" Walking over and placing her hand on his bare chest and placing a soft kiss on his mouth, she lamented, "I'm sorry, I'm just upset! I would love for you to be my support system and accompany me." He kissed her back and said let's get dressed, and I'll make the call.

The two falcons, as they were being referred to now, made it down to the lobby in record time. Abe and Tim were waiting at the desk with the armored SUV on the street directly in front of the door. The drive to the gallery was silent except for Tim and Abe's conversation about the positions that they would assume at the gallery for their two falcons. Marissa was tense, with her shoulders rising as they approached. Max was trying to distract and comfort her to no avail. When they arrived, Abe told them to stay in the car with Tim until he cleared their access to the gallery.

It only took Abe a few moments before he signaled the all clear and Tim opened the rear door. Marissa was out like she had been propelled by a canon. Max watched with concern as she practically ran to the back office. Tim stayed positioned at the front door as agreed, and Abe positioned himself at the office door in the gallery. Max was somewhere in proximity to Marissa, who was ready to hopefully ameliorate Janet's concerns. Her expression was one of pure determination. Going through the remaining orders on the books, Marissa was snapping pictures of each order on her phone to confront Lionel with. She was adamant that they could not lose these important clients because of the FBI's quest for answers. There has to be a better way to handle these interrogations!

Tim came in the front door, locking it behind him. He turned to Abe and directed him to call Lionel immediately. Hearing the *POP POP POP* outside had Abe pushing Marissa, Max and Janet to the floor behind the desk. Each guard had their guns drawn and ready to engage. They were stationed behind the column at the center of the gallery that formed a delineation between the specific art types. After a few seconds of gunfire, everything went silent. Marissa was ready to jump up when Max grabbed her and pulled her behind him. She whispered that the storage room would be more secure and they could access it from the door directly behind where they were huddled. Tim overheard and yelled, "GO NOW!"

Lionel and several other agents pulled up and jumped out of their vehicles, armed and ready. The offending vehicle, which had fired off the drive-by shots, crashed into a mailbox and car at the end of the block. There was no one in the vehicle, but perhaps forensics would be able to pull something from the car. How was this linked to the abduction case? Would Marissa and Max be safer somewhere outside of D.C. at this point? All of these options were now going to have to be discussed.

Forensics dug a slug from the mortar just beside the gallery door. Another was found on the other side of the street from the armored vehicle Marissa and Max arrived in. Evidently, it had ricocheted from the passenger door of their vehicle. One slug was still in question. The agents escorted the two falcons from the gallery with orders to lock it up and head home. Lionel told Tim and Abe he would be over to the penthouse within the hour to make sure the falcons were settled up there expeditiously.

Entering the penthouse was a relief that they didn't know they needed. Marissa's shoulders dropped several inches as she finally relaxed. Max's head was pounding from the stress of our encounter at the gallery. It wasn't more than 30 minutes before the call came for Lionel to be allowed access to our elevator. He even arrived with a couple of bags of Chinese carryout. He claimed a peace offering was needed after our day. Marissa smiled and kissed his cheek. "That wasn't necessary, but oh, how it is appreciated." Abe and Tim accompanied him, so Marissa brought out dishes and a bottle of white wine.

As a tear slipped down Marissa's cheek, she looked up at Lionel and asked if she was going to have to shut the gallery down for a few days. Lionel's comment was, "You are not only beautiful, capable and successful but also psychic!" Everyone laughed and decided to keep things light while they ate. Business could wait until they relaxed a bit.

After a feast of Mu Shu Pork, Orange chicken, Beef and broccoli, Lo Mein, and brown rice, they sat back and sipped wine while Lionel, Tim and Abe drank sodas since they were "On the clock" and wanted to be able to react quickly if needed. Max told everyone to take a seat in the living room and leave the table alone. He would deal with that later.

Lionel sat next to Marissa, taking her hand in his to explain his thinking. "Keeping the gallery open right now puts everyone at risk. We need to get a handle on who was behind today's attack and put some distance between the gallery and the patrons who are being interrogated." Marissa looked at her hands and shook her head in agreement. Her only question was, how would she pay Janet if the gallery was closed? Max immediately spoke up, giving Marissa the option of having Janet come here at least twice a week to help go through the files and organize everything. He offered to cover her salary until things were running again. Marissa's gut reaction was absolutely not! She wouldn't let him pay for her staff. He smiled and told her he wouldn't even notice the amount leaving his accounts and she knew that! She smiled at him and agreed to speak about that later with him.

Lionel said he would have agents go to the gallery, take the art down, and store it in the back with Janet's direction. They could pack up all of her files and bring them here for her to go through over time. That would certainly take her mind off of everything going on if she was busy with those files. She gave Lionel the key to the gallery and said she would coordinate with Janet to meet the agents there. She then agreed that the best course of action was to close the gallery until this chaos was over. Max wrapped his arms around her and kissed the top of her head. "This is difficult, but definitely the right choice," he murmured in her ear. Leaning into him, she kicked off her shoes and brought her feet onto the sofa, tucking them under her.

Max asked Lionel if getting away for a week or so was an option. Lionel chuckled and agreed that it sounded good but made no sense until they had a clearer picture of what and who they were dealing with. Max said he would be willing to pay for the security they would need to take with them when the time came. "Of course," was Lionel's only response. "And, I assume you would use a private plane?" Which caused Max to blush slightly and agree.

Max then shrugged and looked at Marissa, stating, "My investments have made me a great deal of money over the past couple of years. What am I going to do with it? I want to afford us as much comfort and security as possible!" She smiled and relented, kissing him and whispering, "I'll show my gratitude later" in his ear.

As Lionel, Tim and Abe departed to assume their assigned spots, Max armed the security system and bundled her into his arms carrying her back to the bedroom again.

Chapter 20

Sinking into the bubbles in the tub as Max started the waterfall to circulate the warm water, Marissa sighed her pleasure. Max used his business baritone voice to assure her that everything was going to be alright. As he slipped in behind her and fondled her breasts, pinching her nipples, she could already feel his arousal against her spine. Reaching back, she stroked him softly, eliciting a growl. He adjusted his position, lifting her to straddle his thighs and whispered in her ear, "I'll claim my showing of gratitude later; this is just slow and lazy stimulation to show you how much you mean to me."

Smiling to herself, Marissa moved her hips in a circular motion as slowly as she could, resting her head against his chest. She could feel his heartbeat increase as she continued her languorous movements. Holding onto the side of the tub, Max slid further into the water in order to change the angle. They both moaned in unison as she reached behind her to bring his lips to hers. Sliding in and out of her, Max declared something he had been thinking without realizing he said it out loud. "I am falling hard for you, my love." Smiling, she pushed herself down as far as she could, taking him to the point of no return. Holding that position as he pumped with more vigor into her, they both were moaning and writhing against each other when Max said, "God, I love you! Put me out of my misery and say that you will consider marrying me when this is over!" She moaned as her muscles contracted on his point of entry, and she saw an explosion of stars! She reached both her arms behind her wrapping them around his neck as he sucked on her neck, releasing inside her growling.

Asking if she was going to answer him, he sucked on her earlobe and moaned in her ear. She stepped up out of the tub and motioned for him to follow. Simpering, "Yes, I will always be yours, Maximillian Corleone! I love you, too, more than I ever thought possible!" With that response, he bounded out of the tub, dripping over the floor without drying, and chased her giggling down the hallway. As they ran into the living room, they were met with a pair of stunned eyes. Roger had just entered from the elevator as they came around the corner. Bellowing "Holy Shit! I'm sorry!" He turned around as they started laughing out loud. "Well, that is surely an unexpected way to greet a guest!"

After throwing on some clothes, Max went back to greet Roger. "Next time, call or text first, OK Roger?" Roger was still a shade of crimson as he whispered, "Damn man, she is one smoking hot body!" Max admonished him with, "That is my future wife you were ogling, Roger!" Turning around with an expression of total shock, Roger responded, "What? When and how?" Maxed chuckled and said just seconds before you arrived! Roger remorsefully looked in the direction of the bedroom and said, "You SOB! Who's going to be my wingman from this point on?"

Sauntering down the hall wearing a silk robe over a camisole and thong, Marissa said, "You are on your own from now on, Roger!" They all laughed, and Roger apologized again for just showing up. Max said they would have to have a new system installed that would alert Max and Marissa of Roger's arrival from here on out!

Sinking into one of the barrel chairs with Marissa snuggled on his lap and her face pressed into his neck, Max and Marissa brought Roger up to date on what had recently transpired. Roger was taken aback by the magnitude of the attacks. "Being shot at had to have been the scariest experience yet."

Marissa divulged her fear of being locked away in a dark basement was more stress-provoking for her. She admitted that before Max was locked down there with her, she was beginning to question her sanity. Hearing gunshots wasn't nearly as terrorizing for her. Roger looked at her with deep concern and asked if that had been a childhood trauma. Her breath caught as she responded, "What would make you ask that?" Roger just shrugged and said that he would think, unless she had been traumatized by being locked in a dark space, being shot at would take the top spot as the fear factor.

Max then asked if anyone wanted a drink as he rose, placing Marissa on the seat where he had been. She smiled and said she could use a bourbon. Max then fixed himself and Roger a scotch. As he handed her the bourbon, he lifted her back onto his lap. The next question was, "Anyone hungry?" Roger turned to look over his shoulder and replied that it appeared they had just recently eaten. Max, feeling a frisson of embarrassment, looked at Marissa and voiced, "Oops!" They all laughed as Max took the empty plates and containers into the kitchen, dumping the leftover food in the trash. Roger said he wasn't planning on imposing for the remainder of the evening and rose to leave. Marissa commented, "After catching us with our clothes off, the least you can do is have dinner with us." Roger, smiling, said that picture was now an indelible image in his brain! To which Max responded, "Use some whiteout!" They all laughed again as they tried to decide what they would all like to eat.

After delving into the recesses of the refrigerator, it was decided that they would need to have some groceries delivered tomorrow. Then they all agreed a pizza and a movie sounded just right. Flipping through the movie choices, they couldn't decide if they wanted a mystery or comedy. Roger said he didn't care as long as they had ice cream to go along with it. They then turned on a mystery, and Roger scooped out some mint chocolate chip ice cream for himself. Max and Marissa stretched out on the sofa, wrapped in a tangle of limbs, as Marissa softly snored into Max's chest. Roger then questioned Max about his declaration of marriage intent. Grinning from ear to ear, Max explained how it just kind of slipped out while they were in the tub. But, the declaration just felt so right, that he had to have an answer that she felt the same. When she professed her love to him, it was the best thing he had ever heard. Roger chuckled and said with a grin, "Whipped!" Max responded, "Undoubtedly!" Hugging Marissa more closely to him.

By the time the movie was done, Max was sound asleep with Marissa in his arms and Roger was on his way out the door. He rearmed the system as he left, smiling to himself and humming "Another one bites the dust!"

Chapter 21

D.C. at night was always still humming to some extent, never really sleeping. The street lights glistened in the drizzle that was beginning to fall, adding to the seasonal chill late at night. Shifts of the guard were changing. The little toy soldiers were exchanging the details of their time watching over this little piece of the city. People outside were bundled against the incoming rain, hidden behind large umbrellas and upturned collars.

Max was deep in thought, watching the raindrops form rivulets down the massive wall of windows. Even the Potomac was void of activity. Swishing the scotch in his tumbler as a singular drop escaped onto his hand, he cursed under his breath and then licked it from his hand. Marissa was engrossed in the files on her lap until she heard him curse. Asking what was bothering him, she rose and padded barefoot over to him, laying her head against his back while wrapping her arms around his waist. He moaned at the contact and rested his left hand over hers on his abdomen.

Max smiled and said that the puzzle pieces were not complete, and it was really concerning him. The more invested in Marissa he became, the more he was anxious and worried. How could the FBI and Interpol not have things more locked down after all of this time? Where was Malcolm Calloway, and what was his end game? Max voiced his feeling of being logy and weighed down by all of the questions that go unanswered.

Marissa asked if they could dress up and go someplace for dinner and then to the club. She felt a need for a change of environment and feeling fashionable. Max laughed at that and told her she was fashionable whether she was wearing sweats or one of her silk numbers. He then suggested they go to his cousin's restaurant and then the club for a few hours and blow away this funk he was feeling. Of course, he would have to call Abe and Tim and have them bring the armored SUV to transport them; notifying Sergio would be easy.

After making the calls Max felt lighter already with anticipation. He slid into the shower behind Marissa, washing her back and kissing her neck. She asked how dressed she should get, to which he asserted, "Clubwear". Marissa slid out of the shower, wrapped herself in the bath sheet and sauntered to the closet. She settled on a leather bustier with a matching jacket to wear with a pair of silk palazzo pants and her Ferragamo shooties. She liked the way the bustier enhanced her bust and gave the leather a feminine "Bad Girl" look. She accessorized with her diamond and lace choker and simple diamond studs that Max had bought for her to replace those lost when she was abducted.

Making her way to the living room, she bundled the files back into the box and tucked it away behind the sofa. When she looked up, she saw Max wearing a fitted leather jacket over a cream silk shirt, left open at the top to show just the hint of chest hair. He had on a pair of black jeans that hugged his muscular thighs and tight butt, and a pair of dress boots to give him that bad-boy look. She smiled at the memory of seeing his tattoo over his left pec of a compass with the sextant intersecting it that she saw the first time they played at the club. It seemed so out of character from his conservative exterior, but it took her breath away. They were so well matched from the first moment they met. No wonder they found themselves always drawn to each other!

Tim held the umbrella over their heads as they were whisked into the SUV. Abe smiled and commented that they both looked "nasty good" in their leather. Laughing, Marissa thanked him for his comment and blew him a kiss. He recalled that being one of her signature moves when receiving a compliment. Max told the two bodyguards that he expected them to join them for dinner at Fiorino's. They agreed and were on the road in no time. Sergio, of course, had the private room in the back set up for the four of them. Entering the room, Sergio went right to Marissa, kissing her on both cheeks, declaring, "Bellissimo!" He sat with them for a few moments, taking time from the kitchen to enjoy Max's love interest. Max took him aside and asked if he would cater an engagement party at the penthouse in a few weeks. Sergio's eyebrows practically shot off his forehead. He conspiratorially asked if Max was saying he was about to pop the question. Max smiled and declared she already agreed to marrying him sometime in the future. He wants to make it official with a ring. Sergio hugged him and called him a lucky man if that beautiful creature agreed to be his, all in Italian, of course!

Finishing another great meal, Max then told Tim and Abe they would accompany them to the club again tonight. Abe smiled and groaned as Tim elbowed him in the ribs. Max laughed at the camaraderie these two seemed to share. Driving to the club, Marissa began to question their relationship. She wanted to know how long they had known each other and if they had served together. She smirked and said she wanted to hear some stories about their time overseas at some point. Tim began shaking his head negatively, causing her to refine her request to tales without details. He chuckled and said someday.

Entering the club, Marissa blew Brad a kiss at the door. He winked at Max and shot him a thumbs up. The coat room was empty tonight, so "Flame" brushed past some patrons to retrieve a bourbon and a scotch from Gary at the bar. He placed them on the napkins before she even got close and extolled, "Looking as gorgeous as ever, Flame!" She blew him a kiss when arms encircled her waist as the gentleman whispered in her ear, "Tonight's not Thursday!" She swung around, ready to lay the man out, when she realized it was Mark. Max shook his head and told him he was lucky her hands were full, or he would be wearing a handprint on his face. Mark laughed and questioned, "Really?" Max declared that no one touched her without her permission, and he, of all people, should know that! They all then laughed about it and hugged as Mark led them to his table. Mark then noticed Tim and Abe and asked if they would join. They both affirmed that they were working tonight and would be standing over there, pointing to the shadows by the entrance with a view of the floor.

It was great to be out of the confines to enjoy some socializing tonight. But after her third drink, Marissa ran her hand up Max's leg, stopping just short of his package, brushing it with her pinkie, causing him to moan in her ear. Whispering "Feeling a little adventuresome?" Her response was her tongue in his ear, giving him gooseflesh up his spine. He put her jacket over her shoulders and pulled her to her feet. "This night will culminate in our bed with you bound and writhing, my love," he groaned into her neck, just loud enough for her and no one else to hear. Bidding good night to Mark and motioning to Tim and Abe, they made their way to the door.

Tim stepped out first and immediately pushed them back inside, drawing his weapon and locking the heavy metal door. He turned to Abe and said, "Falcons to the nest," signaling to have them whisked into a locked back room as the call was made to Lionel and the police. Marissa's eyes were as wide as saucers, and she clutched onto Max's arm. He withdrew his Glock from inside his jacket, surprising her that much more. As tears slid down her cheeks, she watched everyone go into panic mode while bundling her to safety.

It wasn't until hours later that the story unfolded. Brad was on the ground by the door with blood pooling beneath his head when Tim opened the door. Fortunately, he was only unconscious for a short time when Tim saw him. An ambulance was called immediately for Brad. He was taken to the hospital for observation with a concussion and six stitches to his scalp. He was unable to tell them how it happened since he heard or saw no one but stars when he was hit over the head. Fortunately, the heavy metal door was locked! Therefore, no one could access the club without Brad calling inside for access. When Brad approved the client, he called to the bar with his password-protected app on his phone, and Gary would press a button, allowing the door to be opened from the exterior. This particular form of security was a recent installation by Cyrus and Felix Newcomb, the club owners. There was a concealed camera by the entrance that sent the feed and recorded it in the office. After the area was cordoned off by the police, Max and Marissa were whisked back to the penthouse while the police and agents on the scene watched the video feed to determine the who and how.

Once home, Marissa slinked back to the ensuite to run a bath and removed her clothes before Max even knew where she had gone. Some voice in the back of Max's head told him to check his security cameras. He didn't do it often, but the hairs on the back of his neck were standing on end, and he had a strange feeling. After the events of the night, he needed to feel in control again. Pulling up the feed on his laptop in the office, he sighed with relief when the elevator and lobby feeds were clear. But when he saw the rooftop feed, the blood drained from his face. He immediately called Lionel, Mark, and Jennifer Reed from her unit on the 7th floor, explaining that while they were out, an unidentified chopper landed on the roof pad, and two men jumped out and attempted to gain access through the rooftop door. Fortunately, with Max's insane amount of security, they were unsuccessful and left after about 15 minutes.

Max then ran into the ensuite and stopped Marissa from stepping into the tub. He wrapped her in a robe and instructed her to dress in something comfortable because they would have agents going over the rooftop deck in a few minutes. She asked what was going on, to which he stated that he would tell her once she was put together and in the living room. Before she was even finished dressing, Max was alerted that the agents needed access. When Max brought them up it was the full entourage of FBI security assigned to them. Lionel was followed in by Tim Donelly, Abe Kaufman, Jennifer Reed, Tom

Halverson and David Martin. Mark Winslow was right behind them, wanting to know what was going on.

Max guided them into his office and turned the laptop on, connecting it to a screen that dropped down from the ceiling. Marissa entered after everyone else wrapped her arms around Max's waist and laid her head on his chest, listening for the rhythmic sound of his heart that made her feel more secure, musing to herself that it was like being in utero again. As the screen came to life, the chopper came into view and hovered for a few moments before landing. Without even turning off the rotors, two men in black with balaclava masks over their heads attempted to open the rooftop door using crowbars. There was nowhere on the door for them to get purchase since it was flush and required Max's biometrics to open it. After a few unsuccessful attempts, they hopped back on the chopper and took off.

Lionel turned to his four men and sent them up to the roof to be sure nothing was left behind. Directing them to check every surface and crevice, he turned to Max, asserting that whoever that was knew of the helipad. Max then listed everyone he was aware of that knew of it being there. Lionel then requested a copy of that video for his people to try and identify the chopper since all air vehicles had to display registration numbers prominently. Max led the agents to the rooftop interior door in the master suite and up the stairs to the exterior door that required his retinal scan to open. It was hard not to notice them all taking in the bedroom, art and open closet door that was lit, affording them all a brief view of its interior. Abe, in his inimitable fashion, had to be pulled out of his awe to get to work. Tim just shook his head, smiling. Everyone else was definitely more discreet in their perusal. The susurrus about the art made Max smile and turn to address the agents. "Yes, the art pieces are originals. I inherited them from my parent's estate when they were killed!" Mark then interjected that when they return to the hall, they should check out the photographs of his clientele on the wall. Garnering a scowl from Max over his shoulder. To which Mark remarked, "But keep remarks to yourself. Max is a very private person! Sorry Max, loose lips run in my family!" Max smiled to himself as he continued on. When he opened the exterior door, Tim told him to prop the door open so they could get back in, but he wanted Max to return to the living room just in case.

Alleviating Max's stress was the first thing on Marissa's mind. He was wearing his stress across his shoulders, and she could tell he had a headache blooming by the way he kept rubbing his temples. Gliding across the floor toward the bar, she poured a scotch on the rocks for Max and began to massage his shoulders. His moan brought all remaining eyes in the living room to him. She smiled coyly and dared anyone to comment. He took her hand from his shoulder and drew her face to his, asking if she was trying to get him in trouble. Her lips curved up seductively when she purred, "Later, my love. You are the one who threatened bondage, if you recall."

Once the roof was cleared and the video feed was handed over, Lionel asked if they wanted Jennifer to stay with them overnight. Max smirked at Lionel and responded that the 7th floor was not that far away and they would be fine. Lionel grinned at Max and winked "All right then, a couple of floors between won't deter a quick response if needed." Tom Halverson and David Martin were directed to remain at their posts in the lobby until the morning as they all filed out of the penthouse, leaving Max and Marissa alone again.

Chapter 22

Sunlight filtering through the crack in the drapes in the master bedroom brought Marissa out of a deep, relaxed sleep. She turned to check the time on her phone, when a strong arm wrapped around her from behind and pulled her to his chest. Pivoting in his embrace, she pushed away and slipped beneath the covers, eliciting a moan from Max as her mouth took his hardness in deeply. Humming as she worked him over, fondling his sack gave her satisfaction after all of the attention he gave her after everyone left last night. It felt as though they had just fallen asleep, which actually was the case since they dozed in between orgasmic sessions all night. Max tried to pull her up to him since he felt unable to stop himself if she persisted. Marissa had other things on her mind, though.

As she got him as close as she could without letting him go over the edge, she popped him out of her mouth and began nipping up his body, causing a growl to erupt from his chest. Laying her hand over his erection, she poked her head out of the covers, telling him turnabout is fair play. Waiting to feel his pulsing subside, she dove back under and sucked hard and fast. Max practically lifted off of the bed as he called her a tease and a minx who should expect retaliation. Groaning, he pleaded with her to either ride him fast or suck harder while he tried to hang on to his sanity. She let him go with a pop again as he growled that she was cruel. She came out from under the covers and straddled him as he grabbed her hips and pushed himself deep inside her. Guiding her pace, he was panting with need as she slammed her tight heat as far down as she could and wiggled while she giggled at him. Pinching her own nipples as he struggled to set a pace, she screamed, "Now Max! Oh God, NOW!" as she took him over the edge with her, groaning her name. He looked up at her, unable to put together a coherent thought since that had to have been the strongest orgasm he had ever had. She stayed connected to him until he was completely flaccid as she laid on his body, smiling.

Climbing out of bed to stroll to the shower, Marissa noted the time. They had never slept this late in the morning! Max threw back the covers, determined to join her in the shower. He suggested she have Jennifer join her for a few hours today and possibly invite Janet over to go through the boxes of files. When asked where he was going, the cryptic answer was the need to contact a client in person. Looking away from her, since he was a miserable liar, he said he would have Tim drive him. She agreed to the itinerary and finished showering before making her calls.

Max called downstairs to Tim and set up a meeting at 11:30 in the lobby. He told Tim he would fill him in when he got downstairs. Grinning like a Cheshire cat when the elevator doors opened, Max stepped lively into the lobby, finding Tim engrossed in a conversation with Abe. Not wanting to interrupt, he waited at the security desk until Abe pointed in his direction, and Tim turned around to approach him. "What's up boss?" was the greeting Max received.

Max needed to be sure Tim could be secretive and not disclose anything to Marissa, so he asked for his assurance. Tim explained that he was very tight-lipped when asked to be, causing a huge grin from Max. Tim scrutinized Max's expression and immediately began to smile to himself. He was directed to drive to Market Street Diamonds at 2512 Pennsylvania Avenue N.W. Smirking to himself, Tim questioned the occasion. Max said, "Just drive! You'll see soon enough." Parking directly in front of the building, they anxiously entered the store. Max greeted the designer Dino, who grabbed Max into a tight embrace and questioned why he hadn't seen him for so long. Max laughed and said they had just spoken several days ago at Sergio's restaurant.

Directing Max to the vault jewelry that Max had requested to see, Max was struck immediately by "The ring"! "I want the Cathedral Halo Pave setting right there," he said, pointing to the ring of choice. "I want a perfect 5-carat cushion cut diamond set in it, and I want the pave diamond wedding band that goes along with it." Dino, laughing, said, "Why do you need me then?" Max smiled and declared, "Only you can find the perfect diamond for it and set it for me in a two-week time frame!" Dino smacked Max on the back and said I have the diamond in my vault and can set it for you overnight. She must be someone very special to get you this worked up. Max turned to Tim and said, "Describe her for Dino, please."

"After giving an in-depth description and seeing the look on Max's face, Tim blushed, saying, "What? I appreciate a beautiful, intelligent, capable woman!" Laughing, Dino commented that Max better get that ring on her finger and a commitment fast if that description is accurate! Handing Dino his Black Amex card, Max said, "I will have Tim pick it up in two days then, if that works for you." Smiling as they got back into the SUV, Max asked if he needed to have Tim sign an NDA. Tim smiled at the reflection in the rearview mirror and congratulated Max. He even went so far as to say they were perfect with each other from what he has experienced. Max closed his eyes and rested his head back as they made their way home. Never expecting to marry, he even surprised himself.

Entering the penthouse, Max could hear a trilling laugh and Marissa's distinctive giggle coming from the bedroom. Tiptoeing down the hall to the opened doors, he was taken by complete surprise to find three half-naked women and clothes strewn all over the bed. Clearing his throat, he laughed as they screamed at his intrusion into their fashion show. Jennifer dropped down behind the bed, and Janet grabbed clothes to cover herself as Marissa strolled over, swinging her hips in an exaggerated show of femininity, wearing only a white lace thong and matching bra. He groaned and pulled her to him and into the hall while greeting the others with "Ladies!"

Marissa jumped up, wrapping her legs around his waist and planting a deeply seductive kiss on his lips. He pushed her up against the wall while fondling her ass and told her she was asking for it. She smiled, responding with, "Yes, I am!" Carrying her into the office, he kicked the door closed and unzipped his pants. Moving her thong to the side, he entered her in one stroke. She whispered into his ear, "You're insatiable!" He laughed and said, "You jumped me! Now stay quiet, and I will take you over the edge before the girls notice you are gone."

Putting himself back together, He kissed Marissa again before putting her bare feet back on the floor. She smiled and asked if his meeting went well. Smirking, he affirmed, "Perfectly!" Then he asked if they had gotten any work done or were they just enjoying "girl time". Marissa giggled and shrugged, helping him to appreciate her relaxed demeanor. He realized she needed this reprieve from what life has become for them lately.

Grabbing a bottle of water from the refrigerator, he asked over his shoulder if they had all eaten anything for lunch. Marissa said they hadn't decided on what to order. He told her to find out what they would want, and he would order and set up the dining room for them. She looked up puzzled, and asked if he would join them. He chuckled and responded that he had work to get done and that they should enjoy their "girl's day". He would grab something later.

The ladies came down the hall with their heads hung in remorse which Max chastised them for. He told them he was glad they were enjoying their time together and should probably attempt to get together at least once a week. Marissa agreed that they were enjoying each other's company but should probably try to get Maggie to join in next week. Max went into his office and closed the door, allowing the ladies their privacy.

As he left the office, he overheard a comment from the dining room. Janet asked if Max was her one. Marissa giggled and stated that Max asked her if she would marry him when this craziness was over. Janet's exclamation of "Oh My God!!! What did you tell him?" caused Marissa to laugh out loud, declaring, "I would marry him in a heartbeat whenever he wanted to make us permanent. He really is the love of my life. I've never felt this way about anyone before!" Jennifer's comment that he wasn't hard on the eyes either made them all giggle.

Max continued down the hall to the master bedroom with a grin and a promise that he would ameliorate this situation as soon as he could. Placing a call to Sergio, he solidified the plan to have the engagement party a week from Saturday. He asked Sergio to coordinate with Roger for the numbers and the menu. Max had to sit for a few minutes after that call; his heart was pounding so hard! He planned on officially proposing the day before the party.

Speaking to Roger about coordinating with Sergio was surreal. He then called Lionel and said he needed to know when this whole debacle was going to be over. Explaining that he planned on proposing a week from Friday brought a raucous laugh from Lionel. He coughed and said, "Sorry, but, oh shit, she has you by the balls, doesn't she? I understand your wanting to make your claim on that sweet little piece permanent, but are you sure of this timing?" Max asserted, "That little piece, as you referred to her, is my future wife! I'll ask you to respect her and watch how you refer to her!" Lionel cleared his throat and declared, "Duly noted." Max then told Lionel he was going to invite him for a party on Saturday a week, but was concerned now sharing about how Lionel saw her. Lionel was contrite in his response and agreed to be more respectful. "But, back to where we are in this whole case, it is so convoluted and complicated with being international, and we still don't know who is trying to get to Marissa. I will try to get more information and update you within a day or two."

Just as Max disconnected the call, his phone buzzed again and showed an unknown number. Unsure whether he should answer or not, he reluctantly pressed the accept button and spoke into the phone, "Max Corleone."

There was a pause before the voice on the other end spoke, "Mr. Corleone, This is Malcolm Calloway, and my understanding is my daughter is living with you. I need to get a message to her. She needs to know that she has been part of an international network of black-market gun and sex slave trade by brokering sales of certain pieces of art. The people who run these networks are not happy about the interference by the FBI and Interpol and are out to eliminate those who are interfering with their business transactions. I used her business without her knowing, and now the powers that be have me and Marissa in their crosshairs. In spite of everything that has transpired in our relationship, I love my daughter and don't want to see anything happen to her. She has to be aware that some of those involved are part of the D.C society and are watching her. Please be careful and take care of her."

Then the line went dead. Max immediately contacted Lionel and gave him the number of the caller and a brief synopsis of the call.

He was sitting on the side of the bed, staring at the floor, when the bedroom door opened, and Marissa sauntered in. She looked at Max's ashen face as he raised his eyes to meet hers. She rushed over to him and pulled his head to her chest, asking what had caused such visible distress. He choked and looked up, whispering, "Your father just called me!" She blanched at that and sat next to Max. He put his arm around her and pulled her to him, kissing the top of her head. "I just informed Lionel and gave him the number to trace. Your father wanted me to know that you are in the crosshairs of some unhappy D.C. society that is part of a black-market group being investigated. He was sending a warning that they are blaming you to some extent and that he is cautioning you because he loves you in spite of your past relationship issues."

Marissa Laughed that sarcastic laugh and rolled her eyes. "Like he's telling us something we don't already know! He also has a strange way of showing his love! The only thing he is concerned about is that I don't draw attention to his involvement!"

Max inquired about "Girls' day," bringing a big smile to Marissa's face. She told him she didn't realize she needed that and thanked him for allowing her friends to invade his space. Looking her in the eyes and holding her by the arms, he stated with conviction, "Our space!" Smiling, she conceded, "Yes, Ours! And thank you for that, too." Smiling to himself, he pulled her on top of him and kissed her deeply. Pushing up from his chest, she smiled and declared her hunger just as her stomach growled loudly. He looked directly at her stomach as he responded, "Loud and Clear!" Laughing, they made their way to the kitchen.

Max watched her round derriere poking out from behind the refrigerator door as she bent to see what was inside. Licking his lips, he tried to reign in his constant desire for this beautiful creature. Smiling, she stood up and asked, "Omelettes?" "Whatever you want is fine with me. Grab the butter and any fresh vegetables in the drawer, and I will whip up something delectable in moments." She snickered, causing his response, "What? You don't trust my culinary skills after all this time?" Wrapping her arms around him from behind, she murmured, "Better than mine, that's certain."

After picking a white wine and collecting plates and silverware, Marissa called from the living room. "Informal at the cocktail table in front of the T.V. OK with you for tonight?" He smiled over at her, saying whatever she wanted was fine with him.

Chapter 23

With full stomachs and a bottle of wine consumed between them, Max drifted off to sleep with his head in her lap as she worked her fingers through his hair. The feeling of being dulcified made her smile down at his handsome face in sleep. This man was her everything!

As the movie ended, Marissa was getting ready to wake Max to go back to bed, when an alert flashed across the screen. ***"Breaking News! There has been a fatal shooting in the district after a political cocktail party at the Smithsonian. The photo that was shown was Malcolm Calloway the third!"***

Marissa screamed, and Max jumped to his feet, ready to defend her. Looking around frantically, Max saw her focus was on the TV screen. Her hands were covering her mouth, and her eyes were wide with fear as she trembled in shock! He jumped to his feet grabbing the remote and switching the T.V. off. She melted into his arms as she sobbed, "This can't be right, this can't be, can it?" Sitting on the sofa, he pulled her onto his lap as his phone buzzed and her's started to ring in the other room.

He picked her up and carried her to the bed as she continued to sob. Grabbing her phone and setting it on silent, he undressed her and pulled one of his t-shirts over her head. Making his way back to the office, he grabbed a bottle of bourbon and a crystal tumbler, pouring a healthy amount for her. Appearing to be in shock, she just stared at her trembling hands. Mumbling over and over, "This isn't right, not right at all. I forgive you Papa, I forgive you!" After her second full tumbler of bourbon, Marissa laid her head on her pillow and let her eyes close, finally relaxing in the warmth of the alcohol.

Max slid into the hall, leaving the door open to be able to see her on the bed. He grabbed his phone and dialed Lionel. Answering before the first ring was even finished, Max whispered, "What the hell, Lionel! What do we know?" Growling, Lionel reported that there were cameras everywhere, clear photos of the vehicle and the gunman, security got a tag number, and an APB was already issued. Max asked how they were unaware of Calloway's location with all of the people looking for him. "How was he at such a public affair unbeknownst to them? This is a major screw-up! How is Marissa supposed to feel safe if her father was not even on their radar in town?" Lionel affirmed it was a major mistake! "Heads would roll over this!" Disconnecting the call without saying goodbye, Max groaned to himself.

Contacting Tim in the lobby, Max requested a recommendation of increased security that he would personally pay for. Tim told him to let him make some calls to old special ops buddies and see what he could come up with. Max was adamant that Marissa would have around-the-clock security until this was over. Tim told him to lock up, and when he picked up the ring tomorrow, he would have news for Max to deliver with the jewelry box. Tim's last words were, "Get some rest tonight." Max grumbled. "Easier said than done."

Stretching out on top of the covers, still fully dressed, Max pulled Marissa's back to his chest, breathing in her scent until he fell asleep. During the night, Max was aware of Marissa getting out of bed and running into the bathroom. He ran after her just as she was emptying her stomach into the basin. Holding her hair and rubbing her back in a circular motion, he sat next to her on the floor. Wiping her mouth with the back of her hand, she looked at him wide-eyed and asked if it was all a nightmare. He shook his head remorsefully and held her tight as she let the silent tears fall.

They rocked in each other's arms on the bed until the fingers of pink and purple stretched across the dawning sky. Max went to the kitchen to grab coffee for them. Setting the hot mug of her favorite brew on the nightstand next to her, she tried to give him a smile, but it never reached her eyes. She murmured, "I hated him, but he was all I had left! That doesn't even make sense to me!" Max winked at her, saying "He's not all you have left, baby. I'm not leaving you, ever."

Marissa finally fell asleep in Max's arms, so he laid her down on the bed and tucked the covers around her, enjoying watching her sleep. He wasn't ready to waste the day even though he knew he looked and felt like death warmed over. Tiptoeing out of the room, he grabbed his phone to touch base with Lionel again. Lionel's phone went right to voicemail, which was unusual. Max fixed himself another coffee in the kitchen and, leaning on the counter while savoring his brew, his mind went to all kinds of scenarios for the day. Would this be the catalyst for an all-out assault to get to Marissa, or would those angered by the current events feel vindicated by Malcolm Calloway's death? They had to know that she was being manipulated in this whole thing, not even aware of how her gallery played a part.

Startled by his phone going off in his pocket, Max jumped and dropped it on the floor. Cursing and expecting his screen to be toast, he was stunned that it was whole and still ringing. Caller ID showed Lionel on the other end. Max answered, "Please tell me something good. I need to renew my optimistic view of life!" Lionel chuckled and asked if he could come up with Abe and Tim in about an hour. Max explained that since being up all night, Marissa just fell asleep. As long as they could deal with only him for right now, that would work.

Arriving about an hour and a half later, Max shuffled them into his office and closed the door. Tim observed Max's lethargy and told him he looked like hell.

Laughing, Max said not to compliment him up too much, he would have difficulty dealing with his ego later. They all enjoyed the banter when Tim took a box from his pocket and handed it to Max, lamenting that he almost forgot. Max opened it to make sure it was everything he wanted when Lionel looked over his shoulder and whistled. Tim asked to see it also, and of course, that gave Abe permission to lean in for a peek. Abe was dumbfounded and just coughed out, "Holy shit!" Tim smiled and said it looked like what Max was going for. "Did it meet his expectations?" Max smiled and said he knew Dino would have what he wanted! Tucking the box into the vault behind his desk, Max asked if they could deal with the events of yesterday before he fell on his face with exhaustion.

Lionel threw a manila envelope on the desk in front of Max. "See if you recognize anyone in these photos." After going through the group twice, Max said, "One man seems familiar, but I can't say from where."

Just then, the door creaked open, and Marissa, looking drowsy, whispered, "You know I always thought I'd like to write a thriller one day, not star in one!" Max rounded the desk and took her in his arms, asking if she had slept enough. Her response was, "Never enough, but good enough for now. At least it took the edge off!" Pointing at the photos on the desk, she asked if she could look through them. Lionel was more than pleased to have her go over them a few times. After flipping through half of the pile, she stopped and picked up a shot of a man in the car that was identified at the Smithsonian. "This is Alexander Ovechkin, my father's associate from Minsk! What would he be doing here in D.C.?" "That's a good question!" were the words uttered as Lionel's eyebrows shot up his forehead while observing Max's expression.

"That's the man I thought I recognized, too! But, where would I have ever seen him? He was a financial backer and part of a shell company my father apparently used for buying and selling art." Max looked up and yelled, "Ding ding ding ding!" Digging a file out of the concealed drawers behind his desk, he was rummaging through several folders when he held one up over his head. Declaring that one had the picture that corresponded to Lionel's file! "I was called in as a consulting attorney on a case against the Calloway Gallery several years ago. I uncovered a shell company that the primary firm didn't catch, which gave us the edge, and we overturned the injunction against the Gallery!" Marissa looked at Max in astonishment. "That was you? I was told an outside consultant found our needle in the haystack, but I had no idea that was you!" Throwing her arms around his neck and planting a deeply erotic kiss on him as he ran his hands over her backside caused Lionel and his men to blush as Lionel cleared his throat. Marissa looked over contritely, whispering, "OOPS!" They all laughed, and Lionel directed them out of the office.

Letting Max know David would be in the lobby and Jennifer would be working from the 7th floor if they needed anything else, the three departed. As the elevator door closed, Max threw Marissa over his shoulder and smacked each cheek of her bottom as she giggled and pinched his rear from her upside-down position. He then ran his other hand up her leg and under her thong, giving her an indication of his intent now that they were alone. Moaning, she pleaded with him to hurry.

Marissa could feel her body thrumming as Max carried her down the hall. Once inside the master bedroom, he let her body slide down the front of him, brushing over his erection restrained behind the zipper of his jeans. She dropped to her knees in front of him, unbuttoning his pants and sliding the zipper down using her teeth, eliciting a growl from the back of his throat. Pulling his pants down his legs, she nipped at his thighs and ran her hands over the front of him, stroking his balls as she freed his erection. Max wobbled on his feet as she took him into her hot little mouth. Seeing how tired he was, she pushed him back to a sitting position on the edge of the bed before she licked, sucked, and stroked over his thighs and abdomen, culminating at his cock that she deep-throated as she fondled his balls. Letting him go with a pop, she then sucked on his balls, dragging a "Jesus, Marissa, put me out of my misery one way or another please. It's been a long night, and I don't think I can hang on much longer!" from him. Smiling, she slowly removed her clothing, giving him a striptease as he moaned at her. She slithered onto his lap, seated herself on him with a wicked smile and inquired, "Is Daddy too tired for Mommy to pleasure him tonight?" Rolling her over abruptly, he propped her feet on his shoulders and plunged deep inside her. Pounding into her, he panted, "This is going to be hard and fast!" "Yesss! That's exactly what I need right now!" she whimpered. They both moaned and screamed out each other's names, not caring who heard them, as they climaxed in unison.

Dropping onto the bed next to her, sleep consumed Max almost immediately. She wasn't far behind, curling into him and hearing that comforting thumping in his chest.

Chapter 24

The week flew by with revelations of her father's past business dealings and the concerns about the effects they would have on her and her business. Marissa seemed resolute in keeping the gallery closed until they were cleared of any wrongdoing.

She and Max had developed a comfortable rhythm in their lives and they both were determined to maintain it. The reports from Interpol and FBI were piling up and names were being revealed that caused alarm. As the week dragged on, they decided to take a night to relax and have an intimate dinner served for them at home. Max had hired a chef and servers to present a beautiful five-course French cuisine meal by candlelight. Several dozen roses were delivered and set around the room.

Max had a dress of the most exquisite silk delivered earlier in the day. It was a soft blue off-the-shoulder boho style that floated around her as she walked yet hugged all the right places. A masseuse and manicurist arrived at 11:00 a.m. to treat Marissa to her own personal spa experience at home.

Max had showered and was wearing his dark blue Brioni virgin wool suit and a powder blue silk shirt. He decided to omit the tie and anything under the outfit, knowing Marissa could only wear a thong under her dress.

Tucking the ring in his breast pocket, he was ready for one of the most important nights of his life.

The lighting was adjusted and music was playing in the background. He had put his phone on vibrate and turned her phone off completely. The aroma of the food being prepared filled the room, causing Max's stomach to grumble. He mumbled to himself, "That's surely not romantic." Taking his best Shiraz from the rack, he opened it to breathe and took out two wine glasses. Spinning in the open concept room, he inspected everything to be sure it was perfect.

Seeing Marissa float down the hall toward him took his breath away. She walked up to him, wrapping her arms around his neck and pressing her soft body into his muscular one. She kissed him deeply and seductively. Groaning, he whispered that if she kept that up, he would be having dinner with a hard-on. She stood on her tiptoes to whisper in his ear that she was already wet for him after such a decadent day of pampering. She declared her intent of seducing him later.

Max poured them each a glass of the "Pomerol 2017" shiraz as the escargot was served. Savoring the garlic butter dripping from the shells, Marissa couldn't wait for the next course. Cleansing the palate with a peach sorbet, the sweet-tart duck breast with cherry sauce was placed in front of them on the exquisite china layered on silver chargers. A salad of baby peas and carrots with goat cheese and almonds accompanied the duck. Another tiny serving of sorbet was delivered to again cleanse the palate before an assortment of cheese followed by Chocolate Mousse was presented as the culmination of the meal. A bottle of "Armond De Brignac" champagne was opened and poured into a crystal flute for Marissa as Max drank the remainder of the shiraz.

Rising from the table, Max extended his hand to Marissa, asking for a dance. Taking her in his arms, he knew this was the woman he wanted to spend the rest of his life with. They swayed to the music until the end of the song when he spun her out. As she came back into his body, he dropped to one knee, declaring his intent, "I had no thought of ever being married until I met you! You have haunted my thoughts and dreams ever since that first night at the club. I never want to share you with anyone. Please say you will dedicate your life to me and become my wife." Throwing her head back, laughing, Marissa then leaned over, pulling Max to her as she whispered, "You knew I would say yes. You didn't need to seduce me with such a memorable night! YES, Yes, a thousand times YES!" When Max placed the 5-carat ring on her finger, she gasped and declared her thrill by pulling him to her and jumping into his arms, wrapping her legs around his waist. "Let me show you how much I adore you!" was whispered in his ear as he carried her back to the bedroom.

Max called over his shoulder, "You are free to leave after everything is cleaned up, Raymond! And any noise you hear while cleaning will be from my fiance, so please ignore it!" Laughing, Marissa smacked Max on his butt.

Carrying her back to the bedroom, Max dropped her on the bed and jumped on top of her, causing her raucous laughter. Tearing his shirt over his head after just unbuttoning the three top buttons, it caught at his wrists, impeding his movement. She smiled that devious smile and whispered that he was her captive now, experiencing bondage assisted by his shirt. With him incapacitated, Marissa drew his belt through his belt loops and lowered his pants. Once he was naked from the waist down, the belt was threaded through the shirt and attached to the headboard. Max growled at her as she kissed and licked every inch of his ripped, naked body. She started from his neck, kissing and leaving love marks all over his shoulders. She then began kissing his big muscular arms, starting from his forearms, then to his biceps, and then going on to his underarms, kissing and licking every inch of him. His fresh, woody perfume, mixed with his manly body odour, had Marissa soaking in between her legs. Looking into his eyes with a mischievous smile, she ran her hand gently down his navel and between his legs, and then said to him, "I want to suck every inch of your cock, big boy!"

Spreading his legs and lowering herself between his thighs, Marissa looked at Max licking her lips and teased him by sucking on his balls as he squirmed beneath her. Taking his engorged cock into her mouth, Marissa continued to deep-throat him until she swallowed his release in spite of his complaints. Groaning at his inability to stop himself, he felt spent by the time she lifted her head, smiling and wiping her mouth on the back of her hand. Marissa teased Max with her revelation that it was him that Raymond heard moaning and growling.

After Marissa released his hands, he grabbed her wrists and used his belt to restrain her arms above her head. Reaching into the nightstand, Max retrieved the handcuffs and spread her legs to the extent that he could and cuffed her in a spread eagle position. Reaching into the closet, he gathered scissors and the flogger, laughing as she squealed and pleaded for release from her restraints. He shook his head as he cut the dress and her undergarments from her body. Using the flogger on her body to elicit sensory stimulation, dragging it up and down her body as she squirmed, Max enjoyed her discomfort. He had a sinister expression as he reached for the blindfold, flavored oil and vibrator from the drawer. Climbing up her body, he tied the blindfold on and began a sensual massage with the flavored oil. Using the vibrating device on one breast, he took the other nipple into his mouth, suckling and biting. Making his way down her body kissing and licking the flavored oil as he went, he used the vibrator on Marissa's clit to add to the stimulation. She felt ready to fly as he reached her folds and inserted two fingers, finding her g-spot. "Oh my God Max, this is too much! I need to find a release fast or I may pass out," was her request in a low purring tone. Max worked her to the edge and abruptly stopped. Marissa almost wiggled her way out of her arm restraint when Max entered her with a growl. Unable to control themselves, they screamed their release together. Dropping on the bed next to her, Max was panting with a huge smile as he asked her when she would become Mrs. Corleone.

As they drifted off to sleep that night, Max wrapped her in his arms and legs, breathing into her neck.

Chapter 25

The party to celebrate the engagement was set up while Max and Marissa were enjoying a decadent long soak in the tub. Max washed and massaged Marissa's scalp, extending their time in the bath. Enjoying the warmth and sensuality of the experience distracted Marissa from the sounds and machinations in the open concept area, and Max kept her in the bath as long as he could, with music being played in the suite to cover the sounds in the main area.

Sergio brought the food in and set up everything as quietly as he could, with Roger transporting the flowers and decor up the elevator in shifts. Max put the coordination of the party in Roger's capable hands. Marissa questioned the sounds in the other room once their bath was complete. Max brushed it off as the cleaning crew, trying to distract her.

There was a beautiful dress on the bed again that Max had set out for Marissa. It was a deep green velvet sheath that was form-fitting with one long sleeve on the right side and no sleeve on the left, leaving her left shoulder and arm bare. The slit again was practically thigh high, showing off her deliciously athletic left leg as she walked. Max had conveyed the message that they would be going out tonight, so dress accordingly, to Marissa.

He donned his black Brioni suit and a hunter-green silk shirt sans tie. They were a striking couple!

Hand in hand, they strolled to the living room. Max caught the gasp just before the question rang out, "Maximillian Corleone, what is all this?" Smiling broadly, Max told her it was an engagement party. "Since our travels are restricted, I thought that we could bring everyone to us instead!" taking her in a warm embrace that was reciprocated. Everything was now copacetic!

For the next several hours, they enjoyed great food with good friends. The ice sculpture of a mermaid seated on rocks was the primary focus in the room, but the gorgeous white roses and gypsophila added to the splendor. Even Tim and Abe were free today to join in. The booze flowed freely from the open bar, as did the extensive spread that Sergio brought from his restaurant kitchen. There was ravioli with marinara sauce, Risotto ai frutti di mare, fried calamari, bruschetta, roasted eggplant caponata, Beef spiedini, Focaccia Barese, slow-cooked meatballs, Caprese skewers with fig flavored balsamic, Antipasto, Goat cheese crostini, stuffed dates, Cheesecake, cannolis, biscottis, amaretti, pignolis, and a fruit with a chocolate hazelnut fountain. A string quartet played in the corner as trays were passed around the room. Roger appeared to pair off again with Marissa's best friend, Maggie, while Janet spent the night in an intimate conversation with Abe. No one talked shop, affording a relaxed atmosphere for all. Jennifer and Tim appeared to slip off together halfway through the night with the assumption they were in her 7th-floor apartment. Marissa was planted on Max's lap with him running his hand up and down her exposed leg absent-mindedly. She quite often flashed her ring in the candlelight, smiling coyly as it sent reflective rainbows around the room.

As the party wound down around 2:30 a.m. Sergios' crew showed up to clean up and cart away anything not consumed, which wasn't much. Roger escorted Maggie home, and Lionel ended up camped out on the balcony. Max took a blanket out to him and started up the outdoor heaters without even causing him to stir.

By late morning, around 10:30, everyone had slipped away, including Lionel. Max slipped from the bedroom to make sure he and his fiance were alone before climbing back into bed and ducking beneath the covers to bring his woman to another climax. Starting at her feet, he kissed his way up her legs, paying special attention to those special erogenous zones he knew only too well. Licking behind her knees and nipping his way up her thighs to the junction where he spread her legs, affording him space to wedge his wide shoulders between them. He used his mouth expertly, drawing moans and shivers from her until her first orgasm hit. Continuing to play her like a symphony, he took her over the edge twice more before he couldn't refrain from seeking his own release. Placing her feet against his shoulders he knelt between her legs, holding her thighs tightly as he plunged into her heat growling. By this time, Marissa was on the verge of a scream when he took her over the edge with him, moaning her name.

They spent the remainder of the day in bed dozing, cuddling and reading side by side.

When they were too hungry to remain hidden away any longer, they found an entire meal Sergio had left behind for them in the fridge, just needing to be reheated. Slicing up a loaf of Italian bread and heated plates of an exquisite veal dish with a green salad, they sat in front of the T.V. and devoured the food along with a great bottle of Brunello di Montalcino red. Lounging in each other's arms after a fabulous meal just seemed so right.

It wasn't until much later that night that Marissa realized her phone was still turned off and in the bedroom on a charger. Retrieving it and opening up her texts, she noticed several overseas numbers had texted her. Handing the phone to Max with a look of concern on her face, she inquired about his thoughts on responding to these texts. His brow furrowed, and he immediately sent the numbers to Roger to see if he could trace them before she responded. The speculation about their origin caused a tension in his shoulders he hadn't had for some time and was hoping he wouldn't have again. He honestly believed that part of their lives was done, and he was ready to move on optimistically.

Waiting until the early morning hours for a response from Roger left Max with an almost sleepless night. Were it not for Marissa curled upon his chest, he was pretty sure he would have spent the night pacing and ruminating. Why was their life together one step forward and two steps back at times? This should have been the happiest time instead of apprehension about the constant barrage from outside forces.

Roger reluctantly contacted Max with word of who the number belonged to. It is registered to Malcolm Calloway 3rd! Which is impossible! Unless someone else now possesses some of his property. It was decided that further information was definitely required before there was any response. Max then sent the information to Lionel to keep him in the loop.

It wasn't long before both Roger and Lionel were requesting a face-to-face with both Max and particularly Marissa. Roger stayed in the lobby, waiting for Lionel's arrival before heading up on the elevator. They were greeted by a hot and sweaty couple after their workout in the personal gym. Max apologized for still being in his gym shorts, but he at least added a t-shirt. Marissa, on the other hand, was very distracting in her capri-length Leopard print leggings and hot pink sports bra. Roger had a difficult time not staring at her hot little body. His thoughts were also very distracting as he tried to mentally discern her measurements. "5'6" tall with probably a 36 C or D bra size, about a 29" waist and a perfectly shaped athletic ass with hips measuring about 35" and legs that seemed to go on forever. He had to physically shake his head to clear the lewd thoughts he was getting about his best friend's fiance.

After everyone had a coffee in hand, they sat in the living room to disclose and ascertain the facts. Marissa was wearing a combination of fear and curiosity on her face. Max was just scowling, waiting for the disclosure.

When Lionel said that it appeared the text was from Marissa's sister, she almost fell out of her seat. "Repeat what you said, I think I heard it incorrectly!" was the only response that came to mind. Max grabbed her hand as Lionel repeated that Marissa had a 22-year-old sister living in St. Albans, England, just about an hour north of London.

After adjusting to the news, Marissa excused herself to go back to the bedroom. Max asked if Roger and Lionel could see themselves out as he rose to follow after Marissa.

Chapter 26

Max entered the bedroom to find a stunned Marissa staring out the windows at the bleak view of rain on the Potomac. He wrapped his arms around her, placing his chin on her shoulder, whispering, "A penny for your thoughts". She turned to take his face in her hands. "Did you forget about inflation? It must be at least a quarter by now!" Laughing, they both fell into an embrace, locking their lips together, tongues tangling until breathless.

"I guess I never thought about it, but it makes sense that I would have a sibling out there. I wonder how many more there are! And what nationalities did he impregnate over the years? But, the most important part of this revelation is what is the name and claim to her portion of his estate and has she even been documented by him? I am more than happy to give her what she deserves for putting up with his love or neglect for 22 years."

Max looked into her troubled eyes and asked if she would want to have her sister flown here so she could meet her. Then it struck him: if she was discovered by whoever was hunting them, was her life in jeopardy? Does Interpol have her under their protection, or do they not know she exists? Too many questions to sift through alone! Max placed another call to Lionel to pose these questions to him for clarification.

Going into the master bath to shower together and scrub each other's bodies seemed like just the distraction they needed until Lionel got back to them. Naked and hungry for each other, they blocked out any thoughts of the outside world as the warm water cascaded over their bodies. Max went to his knee and threw Marissa's leg over his shoulder, using a combination of his tongue and fingers to divert Marissa's attention. Working his way up her body after taking her over the edge, he plucked her right nipple causing it to lighten into a peak while he sucked and used his tongue on her left. Grabbing her left nipple between his teeth, he pulled until she moaned. In return, she reached for his balls to fondle and work her way up to stroking and gently tugging on his cock. By the time Max pushed her against the glass wall to enter her moist heat, they were both panting. "Pound it all into me hard and fast!" Marissa begged Max, making him growl into her ear, sending shivers over her body. Chasing their release together, the screams and moans were appropriately loud, since there was no one but them in the penthouse. They didn't care how loud they got.

Turning off the water, Max wrapped Marissa in a fluffy towel and carried her into the bedroom. Setting her on her feet, smiling. Marissa let the towel drop as she pushed Max back onto the bed and grabbed her shibari ropes from the nightstand. After binding Max's arms and legs, she straddled his body and began her tortuous journey down his body from his lips to his neck, slowly kissing everywhere on his torso that she knew would drive him crazy. Allowing him time to recover from their shower tryst, she continued to torture him for at least half an hour in this way.

She used the flogger to gently torment him, causing him to plead for release. She could see he was again as erect as before their shower romp. Digging into the drawer again, Marissa found the cock ring and gently placed it around his cock and balls before tightening it just enough to gain his growly request for her to please ride him before he went insane. Laughing, she climbed onto his thighs, rubbing herself back and forth on his erection and pinching her nipples to stimulate herself. He was trying to arch into her to seat himself when she put her fingers around his neck, gently squeezing as she achieved a ball's deep connection. She rode him expertly until he wailed, "Shit, I'm going to come!" She then allowed her walls to squeeze out every drop as she also achieved her orgasm, dropping onto his chest. After a few minutes, she undid his shibari bondage and kissed him as she also released his c-ring. He pressed her to himself as he vowed his love and kissed her breathless.

Marissa looked down into Max's blue orbs and explained that they no longer have just sex but connect on a spiritual and physical level that has no description. She asserted her love and devotion for him and claimed that she wanted to speak about their future. Dropping onto the bed next to Max, she rose to her elbow on her side, ran her fingers up and down his torso, playing with his dark chest hair and stared at him as she made the statement that they never spoke about having children. Max assumed a position that mirrored Marissa's as he said that he most certainly did want them, and it would be up to her to decide how many. Her countenance shifted into a glowing "Mona Lisa" smile as she leaned in to take his lips softly this time. She then rose and announced that they should dress for lunch.

Rustling around in the kitchen, they put together a huge chicken Caesar salad as Max chuckled and teased, "Someone is very hungry, it seems."

Marissa carried their plates and silverware to the table, and Max grabbed the salad bowl and what remained of their wine selection from the night of the party. The remaining afternoon was spent talking about when they would actually get married and how long they would remain in the penthouse. With that thought on his mind, Max questioned where Marissa would want to live were they to decide on a house in the future. The conversation was light and enjoyable until Marissa brought up how she should deal with the news of her sister.

As the afternoon morphed into the evening, Max called Lionel again to request a sit down to discuss their most recent news and how to deal with it. Marissa called her best friend, Maggie, to touch base with her while Max spoke to Lionel. Maggie recounted her evening with Roger, much to Marissa's surprise. It seems that Roger has been very attentive since the party and is taking Maggie to dinner tonight. Therefore, Maggie had to cut her conversation short to get ready.

Standing in the office doorway as Max terminated his call to Lionel, Marissa looked like the cat that had just eaten the canary. Max looked up and smiled, stating that Marissa appeared to be ready to burst with the news. Giggling, she told him about Roger and Maggie. But she hadn't gotten enough details yet to have a real idea of how serious this was. Max threw his head back and guffawed that Roger was now feeling left behind since they announced their engagement. Not knowing Maggie very well, he had no insight into how this pairing would progress. But, he did assert that Roger, underneath his public persona, was a really caring and sensitive guy. He would make a wonderful boyfriend to the right person, adding, "And maybe that person will turn out to be Maggie."

Shifting into his attorney persona to do research online, he called Marissa over to the cocktail table, where they folded themselves onto the floor with their computers. Digging into who this Amanda Calloway was and her background gave them both a new purpose for the hours ahead. Max began digging into her work profile and where exactly she lived, while Marissa began with her possible online profiles and the quest for a photo to identify her. Together, they compiled an extensive dossier on this "little sister". Printing everything they were able to turn up, they began to put things in chronological order and make a lifetime profile book if possible. Marissa was focused on the most current photo she could find. Asking Max if he saw any resemblance, while she held her breath for the answer made her feel like she was about to hyperventilate. Max squeezed her hand and asked what her concern was.

Shaking her auburn waves and looking up with moist green eyes, she claimed that she had always wanted a sibling to grow up with. "Finding one as an adult is… confusing. Do I want to have her in my life at this point in time?" she said to Max.

Their intimate time giving attention to the issues of the day was cut short by a call from Lionel, who was in the lobby. Max directed Marissa to change into something that didn't show all of her assets to Lionel. Looking down, she recognized his concern since her breasts were on full display in the sheer camisole, and her little silk sleep shorts didn't cover much either. Running down the hall, she appreciated Max's concern and decided to throw on some yoga pants and a T-shirt while Max escorted Lionel to the penthouse.

Standing in the kitchen retrieving another bottle of wine from the cooler, she heard them before she saw them. Eavesdropping on their conversation as they made their way toward the living room, Marissa asked, "What house are you talking about?" Lionel chuckled, stating that she had excellent hearing. He then repeated his story that he found the address for Amanda, and also found that the cottage she lived in was paid off several years ago when her mother died. "She has lived there since she turned 18. It appears your father was very generous with her. She lives modestly but comfortably. She is employed at a flower shop, which your father invested in for her, so she will always own part of it and enjoy an income as long as the shop is profitable. So, as you can see, she is not destitute or without an income. The question now becomes, do you want to reach out at all or just live your life as she lives hers in England?"

Max then showed Lionel what they had been working on earlier, asking what the status is of Malcolm's body, and where he will be interred. Lionel explained that his body was at the morgue currently, and that an autopsy had been performed. What they had been able to uncover from his papers that were retrieved from the Mykonos Villa was that his wish was to be cremated and his ashes spread in the Mediterranean. "My next question will be how involved you want to be, Marissa? You are named as the owner of the Mykonos villa and everything within its walls. The problem being that we can't allow you to go there until we know this network hunting you has been shut down. Your safety is still our primary concern, and that bleeds over onto Max now that you are engaged."

Max asked if it was just a matter of her name being tracked. That could be remedied by them marrying sooner rather than later. Lionel laughed and responded with his explanation, "They have photos of both of you since you have been followed for over a year now." Marissa was shocked by that statement. "A year, how can that be?" "The dealings with your gallery have been going on for longer than that, I would expect", Lionel mumbled, shaking his head. "We just don't quite know the extent of this web yet. Interpol has been following this for at least 3 years!"

Marissa sat down heavily onto the floor, putting her face in her hands and began to sob, "This may never be over!" Max dropped down next to her and grabbed her chin to have her look into his eyes. "We will get through this together. You can't lose hope."

Chapter 27

Marissa asked Max if he would make arrangements for them to go to the Club tonight. She declared the need for some kind of outlet outside of the penthouse. Max deferred to Lionel, who said he would arrange security for 9:00 p.m. until they close. The armored SUV would be available for them, and at least Tim and Abe would accompany them. Turning to Max, Lionel reported under his breath that he would have two other agents there as well since their last outing to the club was compromised.

Max escorted Lionel to the elevator and asked if the Club was secure enough for Marissa at this point. "We will make sure it is!" was the last word uttered before the doors closed on Lionel.

Placing a call directly to Cyrus and Felix Newcomb, the club owners, Max secured the "Red Room" for them at 10:00 p.m. An unopened bottle of Scotch and Bourbon would be placed in the room for security—no surprises this time!

Marissa was in the bathroom when Max entered the bedroom. He knocked softly and entered through the cracked open door. She was looking in the mirror, putting on her make-up, when he came up behind her, wrapping her in his arms and putting his chin on her shoulder. "Whatever makes you feel better, just ask" She smiled that seductive smile and whispered that she needed something for a big release of tension. Chuckling, he responded that she was just insatiable.

Dressed in his black leather blazer over a black cashmere turtleneck and form-hugging jeans, Max waited in the living room for Marissa. When she entered, she took his breath away. The red leather bustier over black silk trousers that floated around her legs but hugged her butt was accented by a form-fitting velvet blazer that left nothing to the imagination. Every curve of her body was wrapped in sensuous luxury. Her breasts were pushed up in the red leather, accenting her cleavage. Her hair was pinned up in a loose chignon with tendrils falling around her face. The only jewelry she wore was her engagement ring and a red leather choker. Her signature red stilettos were on her feet again as she walked in with an air of dominance that he hadn't seen for a while. Smiling, he rose and took her red lips in a bruising kiss before wiping off the lipstick and opening the elevator door for her.

Driving to the club in silence, Max sensed an electricity between them. Anxious to explore more of their connection tonight, he placed his hand on practically at the apex of her thighs and squeezed. Coyly smiling to herself, she reached over and cupped his groin, giving it the slightest bit of tension as she purred, "You will be my captive tonight. I feel the need for control." He cleared his throat and removed her hand, stating that he would not be able to get out of the car if she continued.

Tim jumped out ahead of them, opening the back door. Bart was again at the entrance to the club as Marissa ran her hand over his cheek, expressing her relief that he was feeling better and back to work. He blushed and thanked "Flame" for her concern. Max nodded at Bart and grabbed her left hand displaying her engagement ring as he kissed her hand and led her inside. She smiled and whispered in his ear, "You can piss a circle around me to exert your dominance if necessary!" Throwing his head back and laughing, he exclaimed, "That can certainly be done!"

Flame waved to Gary at the bar as she sauntered by. Noticed him grabbing their unopened bottles of Angels Envy and Macallan and having them sent back to the "Red Room" with tumblers and ice. Noticing all eyes on Flame again as she removed her velvet blazer, Max smiled to himself. Turning the corner to head down the hallway, he noticed Mark Winslow seated with a blonde at the observation window. He nodded in recognition as they continued down the hallway. As "Flame" opened the door using her keycard, he pulled her back to his front so she could feel his excitement and readiness for their evening, whispering in her ear, "Ladies choice".

Setting the lighting and sound system felt like "home" for Marissa. Throwing open the closet doors, she smiled and perused the space like she had never really paid much attention previously. She looked over her shoulder, inspecting the equipment in the room; she felt giddy. Max just stood behind her with a satisfied look on his face, eyebrow raised in question. The anticipation had her flushed and already wet. He whispered in her ear, "The pheromones you are emitting are out of this world! You are driving me crazy, my love!"

Peeling her pants off, leaving only a red thong and her bustier on, Marissa gave him that Cheshire cat grin and threw her pants at him. "I am so wet, I can smell the excitement! Get your clothes off while I select some toys," she instructed, pulling out the whip and tickler, the bionic stroker and the vibrating butt plug. Looking further into the room, the vibrating saddle caught her fancy along with the obedience chair. Max grabbed the nipple clamps and massage oils for later when things calmed down a bit. Marissa was obviously ready for some heavy-duty tension release!

Directing Max to the obedience chair, she strapped him in. Using the whip and tickler on him to get the stimulation going, she even ran it over herself for the visual stimulation, making him moan. Dropping her bustier on the settee and attaching the nipple clamps, she teased him with her thong by dropping it onto his chest while he was restrained. He breathed in her jasmine and sexual arousal scent, smiling. She then inserted the vibrating butt plug and attached the bionic stroker setting it on its slowest setting as he groaned. "You're not allowed to come until you have my permission, mister!" she told him. Marissa then mounted the vibrating saddle within his view to taunt him that much more. She rode it, moaning, "Damn, I want you so much right now! But you better hold out until I'm done having my way with you, big boy!" Between the butt plug and the stroker, she knew she was making him crazy. But she also knew that the most important part of these toys was to stimulate to an extreme while holding off release. When Max said he couldn't hold it off any longer, Marissa turned off the stroker and vibration until he was calmer.

After compounding this stimulation at least four times more, she could see he was beyond controlling himself. She removed the stroker and climbed onto Max's lap, straddling his thighs and slowly lowered herself onto his swollen erection. Never having experienced him quite so swollen and out of control, she enjoyed the sadistic pace until he was pleading with her to stop the vibrating butt plug and let him come. She smiled as she increased her pace, riding him until they both exploded in a frenzy of light and sound. "Oh God! That was by far the strongest and longest orgasm I have ever had!" Max claimed.

Unstrapping him from the obedience chair, she removed the butt plug and dropped it into the can next to him. He grabbed her and told her the next time they visited this room, she would be the recipient of her tantalizing equipment. Until that time, he would be dreaming about all of the things he would do to her. She purred that she would be looking forward to that time. Meanwhile, he grabbed the oils and told her to lay herself out on the bed.

His massage started as a gentle touch with his hand wrapped around her neck and proceeded down, pinching her nipples as he pulled them using his thumb to alleviate the burn. Running his index finger in a line between her breasts, Max massaged over her hips to her gluteus maximus, lifting her knees for access to the tight little muscle of her anus as he inserted one finger, causing her to purr. Massaging his way over her thighs, pushing them apart without getting close to the bundle of nerves she was desperate for him to touch. There wasn't an inch of her body he hadn't massaged with the oil as she writhed on the satin sheets. Loving the sounds he could elicit from her, he then rolled her onto her knees and entered her. As he smacked her cheeks, they reddened, giving her the pain-to-pleasure experience she deserved.

Opening their bottles and pouring a large amount of scotch and bourbon, respectively, they toasted their evening outside of the penthouse together. Savoring the burn as it slid down his throat, Max turned to Marissa and asked when she wanted to tie the knot. She licked her lips and leaned over, pressing her breasts to his chest and running her tongue around the shell of his ear as he shuddered. She smiled and said, "Yesterday, if all of our days from here on out can be like this." He responded with, "How do you want to do it? At home, in a church, on a beach, a large ceremony, or an intimate one?" She responded with a quizzical look and a shrug. "How do you see it happening?" Max gave her a sly smile and said, "Naked in here!" She swatted his hand and laughed. "Wouldn't that set some tongues wagging!" Hugging her tight, he revealed his wish for it to be sooner rather than later. She asked if there was a particular reason for that, to which he responded that he was thinking about her round with the next Corleone generation cooking. Giggling, she smiled and kissed him again. "We don't have to be married for that to happen. Just say the word, and I will stop drinking and taking the pill." He used his deepest baritone to say, "Now, there's nothing stopping us, is there? That would also give our confinement more purpose!"

Marissa's intent was to go home, throw her pills down the toilet, and let nature take its course. Anticipation of the fun they would have in trying to get pregnant made her flush. Max looked at her devious expression and asked what had just crossed her mind. "Procreation" was the one word that came to mind.

Dressing to head home, they were unable to keep their hands from each other. It took them more than an hour to finally vacate the room. As they walked toward the front door, Max motioned to Tim and Abe so they could get the vehicle set for their return trip to the penthouse. Tim and Abe tried to keep their minds on their duties as they listened to moans and giggles coming from the back of the car. Tim turned the radio up to drown out the hedonistic sounds.

Pulling the vehicle into the garage and up to the private elevator door, Tim said the hairs on the back of his neck were standing on end. He pulled his weapon and instructed Max and Marissa to stay locked inside. Abe began backing out of the space as gunfire erupted around them. Tim reached over the seat and shoved Max and Marissa to the floor as Abe used his skills to extricate the vehicle from the garage. Hitting the speaker button on the dash phone, he used his code name and demanded backup. The blue jackets descended in record time, flushing out the gunmen. One was winged, but one met his end. Neither had any identification on them, causing that sinking feeling again. Hopefully, they would be able to get information out of the one injured gunman.

Lionel then had Max and Marissa whisked upstairs under the protection of four special agent guards until they were again secured in their ivory tower. Shaken but not deterred, Marissa asked if they were again back at square one. One guard revealed hearing that the one gunman who was injured spoke with an accent. Max asked if it was Russian before realizing they would not reveal that to him.

Chapter 28

Marissa and Max settled onto the couch, waiting for Lionel's request to come upstairs. Marissa laid across the sofa with her head on Max's lap, drifting off when Max's phone buzzed. She was startled awake, knowing it was probably Lionel. One of the four agents, still standing at the door, volunteered to take the elevator down and bring Lionel up. Max explained that the elevator would not leave the lobby without either his thumbprint or iris scan. Two agents rode down with Max while the other two remained with Marissa.

Getting off of the elevator as Lionel stepped on, the agents remarked on the security Max had installed, giving him a thumbs up as they left. Lionel stepped on with Max and rode up silently until they reached the penthouse. Stepping off, he released the other two agents while Max poured a tumbler of Macallan Scotch for himself and an Angel's Envy Bourbon for Marissa. Asking Lionel what he would want to drink, he surprised Max with the request for a scotch and water on the rocks. Smiling, he said, "Off the clock now."

Staring into his tumbler of scotch and swishing it in a circular motion until he had his thoughts together, Lionel reported the one gunman who was injured sang like a bird on the ride to the hospital. He was young and, fortunately, inexperienced. Fearing incarceration for the remainder of his life, he opted for Witness Protection. Lionel explained that the kid was a nephew of Alexander Ovechkin and was only 20 years old. He had come to live in the States 2 years ago and was called up by his uncle as backup for the other gunman who didn't make it. The kid was so scared that he was rattling off names and places like he was a tour guide. He admitted that he knew Nicholai Brezinski, who had been taken into custody several weeks ago. He told all about his experience with the black market sex trafficking here in the States and how there were several high-ranking officials here in D.C. that were involved in making good money with kickbacks. He was prepared to put names and faces together for the FBI and Interpol databases. He was to be transported under heavy guard to the main offices for a videotaped disclosure of all he knew. Lionel then looked up and smiled at Marissa, explaining that if all went as expected, this whole debacle should be wrapped up in no more than three months. As names were being disclosed, arrests around the world were being made. But these next three months will be the toughest for Max and Marissa due to their peripheral involvement and fear ramping up within those involved.

Max questioned what that would mean for them. The response was simple and concise. "Stay home!" "You are very secure here. Anything you need can be brought to you here. It is also recommended that Janet Mayfield be contacted and instructed to remove the art from the gallery with the help of agents to be stored in a secure location of your choosing. The gallery has been linked to this trafficking ring through your deceased father's doing. It will be vulnerable to attacks. So, to protect your investment in your business, it is suggested you move swiftly. Just let me know how you want to handle this."

Yawning, Marissa asked if they could review this more later in the morning since it was already 4:20 A.M. Noon was agreed upon for their renewed brainstorming. Lionel departed with a relaxed smile this time.

Naked and exhausted, Max and Marissa climbed into bed together and immediately fell asleep. They were so tired that Max forgot to close the light-blocking drapes. Therefore, the first rays of sunlight split the depth of darkness in their room, causing Marissa to pull the covers over her head and turn into Max's side as they both groaned. Hitting the remote to close the curtains, Max set his phone alarm for 11:00 just in case. When Marissa stirred at 10:40, Max pulled the covers over his head as he slipped between Marissa's legs to wake her in his own intimate way. Moaning and writhing, she woke with a satisfied grin and ready to reciprocate the morning wake-up routine. Max reminded her they had to shower and prepare for Lionel's arrival. Marissa shot him that seductive look over her shoulder as she slid languorously from the bed. Watching her firm, round ass wiggle as she walked to the bathroom, he jumped up and was ready to "save hot water" as they entered the shower together.

Marissa soaped Max's chest and rinsed it as she fell to her knees and took him deeply in her mouth, fondling his balls in her hand. Max groaned out her name as he moved to speed up the process. He fucked her mouth hard until he filled her throat with ribbons of morning cum while moaning her name. She grinned up at him and rose, using his thighs for support. Taking her mouth in a bruising kiss before shampooing her auburn locks and holding her back to his chest, fondling her breasts. He whispered, "Damn woman, I love you so much! How did I get so lucky?" She smiled and responded with her own declaration of love. She then told him she was flushing the rest of her pills this morning since they would have 3 months sequestered here in the penthouse to make something happen. Looking over her shoulder and winking, she exited the shower.

Dressed in leopard print leggings and a black alpaca off-the-shoulder sweater and barefoot, Marissa crept into the kitchen as Max shaved. With coffee made and plates, napkins and toppings ready for the hot bagels she ordered, she sat waiting for the men to arrive. Roger came up, after texting Max about his arrival, with Lionel, Tim, and Abe. Seated around the dining table, they enjoyed breakfast, or lunch, depending upon what schedule you were on, before they settled into business.

Marissa had outlined the pieces that she knew of in the back storage room of the gallery and her recollection of the gallery pieces still displayed throughout the floor.

Calling Janet and requesting that she come over with the inventory book, they brainstormed on the best means of storing the collection. Roger offered his temperature and humidity-controlled storage at Mac Technologies, which would be ideal if it could accommodate the size of the collection. Transport would require packing and crating the pieces for safety, and that would require hiring some pros to come in to pack. Marissa knew of two professional packing companies, but Lionel said everyone working with the art had to be vetted and undergo background checks. Marissa looked up quizzically as he explained there may still be some "Coded" pieces in the inventory and they couldn't risk losing a piece to inform anyone in the "network" where they would be.

Shaking her head with the thought of how convoluted this process would be, Marissa slumped back in her chair. Tucking her feet up under her and reaching over to squeeze Max's knee, she asked if they had someone in mind since they must have had to deal with art before in a case.

Her phone rang with Janet's name showing on the screen. Marissa jumped up, ready to take the elevator down for her, when Max asked Tim or Abe to accompany her. He was being paranoid after their past experiences where she was concerned. Roger suggested that they temporarily add at least two agents to his elevator security scanning system. Max readily agreed, allowing Roger to set it up for them. Once Janet was in the penthouse, Roger scanned Lionel and Tim to allow them emergency access.

Janet and Marissa slid onto the sofa in front of the cocktail table to peruse the inventory logs. With the books spread across the entire cocktail table top, Marissa was surprised at how many pieces she forgot were in the back. There were some rather large pieces that would require crates being built just for their safety. Max handed her the laptop she normally used and suggested she keep her own inventory there as they went over the pieces. Janet had some pieces marked as possible sales to some D.C. Socialites, which Marissa documented separately as part of a list she would hand over to the FBI. It was suggested that someone with the equipment needed to find the elaborate coding carved into the frames present before anything was packed. This process was becoming more complex instead of easier as they established a protocol.

Lionel leaned over the back of the sofa, staring at Marissa's laptop screen and groaned at the process. He then suggested they just have Janet meet his people at the gallery and tag everything as he had his people pack it up. A simple concept that might work more easily. Marissa threw her hands in the air and shouted, "Why must this be so complicated and frustrating?" "It's yours to deal with!" Looking over at Janet, she uttered, "Sorry honey, but you will have to oversee the process and let them in. Just find out the timing, and they will do the muscle work." With that settled, Marissa stood and stretched out her body, drawing everyone's attention to her firm, round ass in those skin-skimming leggings as Tim choked on his coffee. Max chuckled to himself and rose to take refill orders.

Janet packed up her things and said she would be at the gallery to open it for the men tomorrow morning at 8:00 A.M. Max led her to the elevator and escorted her down to the lobby. Experiencing some relief, Marissa excused herself to go stretch out in the bedroom. The men could hash out any other details without her. This whole ordeal gave her a massive headache.

Shedding her clothes, she climbed into bed and snuggled her nakedness into the cool sheets, sighing. She couldn't even remember her head hitting the pillow before she drifted off. The sound of Max opening the door to check on her two hours later didn't even register. When she felt his arms draw her naked body into his, she smiled to herself and wiggled her ass against his partial erection, causing him to groan and harden at once. Looking over her shoulder and smiling, she asked, "Sleep or Screw?" He laughed and said, "What do you think?"

The rest of their evening was a relaxing repetition of dozing, making love and eating. Not necessarily in that order, and some of the eating didn't involve food! Completely satisfied and just a little sore, they added a soak in the tub around 10:00 P.M. Marissa made a production of emptying her birth control pills down the toilet and laughed, saying she hadn't taken any since they talked about it the other night. Laughing, Max stated, "So you could already be knocked up with a Corleone bun in the oven?" She just shrugged and giggled.

The reports of the gallery being packed up were relayed for three whole days until the building was locked up and lights extinguished. Marissa couldn't believe the relief she felt from not having to worry about the gallery or art. Roger phoned each night to check on the progress and how she was doing. He reassured her that the vault where the art was stored was climate-controlled and extremely secure.

Max had a trainer come in and work with him and Marissa twice a week and a masseuse that same afternoon. He had the cleaning people coordinated to be there when they had their training sessions so they weren't disturbed. They enjoyed sitting on the rooftop deck, snuggled up in blankets with the propane heater going and soaking in the tub every afternoon. It was even decided that when they were able to travel again, they were going to marry somewhere tropical with just their closest friends in attendance. Life was finally feeling within their control again.

Chapter 29

At least three weeks had passed before there was another report from Lionel. This time, it was concerning Marissa's sister in St. Albans, England. She had been flying under the radar for months. It was amazing that no one paid any attention to another person named Calloway until two days ago. Interpol had visited Amanda questioning her relationship with her father. When she explained that they hadn't spoken in years, he just made sure there were funds in her account remotely, which raised a few eyebrows. Lionel reported that she had hopped on a flight to D.C. yesterday, and they were tracking her movements.

Amanda texted again, trying to get a response from Marissa, *"I am here in D.C. and was told to seek you out if there was ever any problem."* The second text came in 20 minutes later: *"I desperately need to speak with you. Please meet with me!"*

Marissa was awakened by the persistent dinging of her phone's text tone. Turning to grab it, Max wrapped her in his arms and told her to ignore it for now. Marissa had some other things on her mind now. She smiled smugly to herself that she had not bled since stopping her birth control. She had not said anything to Max yet since it could just be her body adjusting to the withdrawal from the pills.

The phone's notification sounded again, so Marissa reached over and looked at the message from 2 minutes ago: *"Please, I need to speak to you in person! I won't bother you if you would just meet with me. I'll be out of your life forever if you could just talk to me now! I flew all the way across the Atlantic to meet you!"* Feeling guilty, Marissa handed her phone to Max to read the messages and asked what she should do.

Max groaned when he read her texts and suggested they call Lionel and run it by him. Placing the call, Lionel said he would be right over, so Marissa responded that they could meet here in an hour. When she attempted to give Amanda the address, she said she already knew where to go. Marissa shook her head, thinking, *I should have known that if she had my phone number.*

After throwing on a pair of black pants, her fuschia cashmere turtleneck and fuschia ballet flats, putting her hair in a high ponytail, Marissa went to the kitchen to put coffee on. Max was right behind her. He had just ordered pastries and called Lionel back, asking if he would pick them up on the way. Setting up the coffee table in the living room, Marissa decided on a more intimate setting for meeting her sister.

Amanda was at the security desk when Lionel arrived. He walked to her and introduced himself. She was shocked that he would be part of this meeting but resigned herself to the fact that her sister didn't know her and wanted the safety of numbers. Accepting his proffered hand and his card, she followed him to the elevator as the doors opened to Max standing in front of them. Offering her his own greeting and explaining who he was, they ascended to the penthouse.

Meeting her sister for the first time was awkward at best. They both seemed in a quandary whether to hug, shake hands or just go with a nod. You could tell they were checking for resemblances. Amanda's countenance was of total shock as she took in her surroundings. Marissa addressed the fact that Amanda had her green eyes and was her height, but the resemblance stopped there. Amanda had long brown hair and certainly had more meat on her than Marissa. She did look like their father though.

Max told her to make herself comfortable and asked if she wanted anything to drink and a pastry. Amanda smiled and sheepishly asked, "Tea?" Of course, not thinking British, there was no tea. But that could be easily remedied. Putting on the kettle and dragging the box of tea from the pantry, Max asked if she had a preference. Amanda smiled and said any black tea would be fine. Lionel and Tim had already helped themselves to a mug of black coffee. Marissa stated she would like a decaf tea if there was any, making Max do a double take while smiling at her.

Max sat and began the interrogation while the tea steeped. Amanda said she was Malcolm's 22-year-old daughter living in St. Albans, which they already knew. She then launched into the story of her life there. She only met her father a couple of times when she was very young. Her mother had breast cancer and died when she was 18. That was the only time she heard from him again. He bought the cottage she now lived in, invested in her place of work so she was part owner, and deposited into her bank account regularly so she had a nest egg. She said there was a letter delivered to her when he died that told her to reach out to her "sister" in the States if anything happened to him. She was then visited by Interpol and questioned about her father. Confused and saddened by this turn of events, she hopped on a plane to meet her sister, as directed, and find out what this was all about.

Marissa asked if she ever had previous knowledge of family here in the States. Amanda looked up with tearful eyes as a tear ran down her right cheek and lamented that she knew nothing but her quiet existence in St. Albans. Finding that she had a sister after all these years was as much a shock to her as she believed it was for Marissa. Going to sit next to her sister, Marissa took her into her arms, and they cried as they hugged. The room was silent except for the sniffles they shared. All of the men seemed very uncomfortable with the shared emotions in the room. Max jumped up from his seat and asked if anyone else needed a drink. Lionel looked at him with astonishment, stating, "But it's only 11:15 in the morning." "I don't care. I need a scotch!"

As time progressed, Amanda learned of her father's background and holdings, as well as his flaws. Unaware of anything nefarious, Amanda seemed sincere in her angst hearing about it. Marissa even told her about her abduction and Max's to give her some insight. Halfway through the story, Amanda looked over to Max and asked if that drink offer was still on the table. Laughing, Max asked what she wanted. After making her a tall vodka and orange juice, they continued their tale. After about an hour of ping-ponging the narrative between those present, Lionel stopped to ask her if she needed a respite. Shaking her head, she asked if she could use the restroom.

Everyone else in the room looked at each other, puzzled. Marissa directed her inquiry to Lionel, whispering, "What do you make of this?" He explained his feelings that she was for real and had no idea about the circumstances.

When she returned, Max asked "Where are you staying, and how long will you be here?" Amanda responded "I only planned on being here for three days at the Arc Hotel on New Hampshire Avenue." Max offered "You can always stay with us, if that wouldn't be too uncomfortable." Amanda thanked him but said "I only have one more day here, so I'll stay where I am." Marissa chimed in to ask, "Will you come back for a longer visit sometime in the near future? I would love for you to at least stay for dinner tonight!"

Lionel and Tim excused themselves, saying, "We'd be only a phone call away if needed." Max walked them to the door and thanked them for their availability at a moment's notice. Lionel chuckled and said that was their job, but they did find them most gracious hosts with all they had to endure. Lionel inquired how Max intended to handle the will reading. "That's what Attorneys are for," was his response. Lionel and Tim both did a double take, and Tim asked, "Aren't you an attorney?" Max smiled and said, "On an extended vacation!" Tim mumbled under his breath, "Must be nice," but Max overheard and said, "Yeah, it is," causing Lionel to elbow Tim in the ribs as they entered the elevator.

Returning to the living room, Max smiled at the picture of two women who never knew of each other's existence until just recently. Seeing them sitting on the edge of the sofa, facing each other knee to knee and holding each other's hands as they spoke gave him a warm feeling, thinking there would be a family member for Marissa to share with. Knowing how important that will be for Marissa when they have children brought back Marissa's choice of decaf tea earlier. He will have to talk to her about that later. But, for now, he excused himself to go back to his office. He found it cute how they never even looked away from each other to acknowledge his absence.

In the back of her mind, Marissa was cataloging all of the things she wanted to discuss with Max that night. *Would she relinquish her claim to the Mykonos villa? What about her father's financial holdings, how would they be split?* Her mind was running through so many scenarios as Amanda was speaking that she felt embarrassed for missing some of the things Amanda was concerned about. Interrupting her query, Marissa said she needed to visit the restroom. Passing Max's office, she motioned for him to join Amanda while she was indisposed. She knew she enjoyed her father's largesse but had no idea how to broach the subject with Amanda. Money is always a tricky subject when you are not very familiar with the other person's life.

Max asked Amanda if she would like to see some of the photos that Marissa had of her father. So, by the time Marissa returned, Max and Amanda had their heads bent over the "family" album. Calculating the time span, Marissa realized that her father had two families at once. She had no idea if he had even married Amanda's mother or just gave Amanda his last name. A spark of jealousy hit as she thought of how she hadn't had a caring father for so many years. His relationship with her was always contentious, and his money was never given to her freely. What she had after college, she built on her own. Her father never funded her business; instead, he tried to undermine her success. Taking a few deep breaths before sitting down, she composed herself and smiled at Amanda. It certainly wasn't Amanda's fault that he was such a dick to her.

Max looked up at Marissa and asked if she was alright, since the blood seemed to have left her face. Sitting down heavily next to him, she responded with simply an "Uh huh." The next thing he knew, she was falling against him as she blacked out. Amanda jumped up to get her a glass of water as he laid her down, elevating her feet. Coming to with both of their concerned faces above her, she apologized for her "silliness." Stating that she must just have low blood sugar, Max raised his eyebrow and suggested she lay down for a bit. Amanda said she would leave so that Marissa could rest, causing Marissa to plead for her to stay.

Max suggested they order some food for an early dinner or late lunch. Marissa smiled and asked if Amanda liked good Italian food. Max picked up on her suggestion and had a smorgasbord ordered from Fiorino's. Sergio brought it to the penthouse personally, inviting himself for dinner. By the time they finished eating while enjoying light conversation, Amanda begged to be excused since she was still on European time and was feeling the time difference. Sergio offered to drive her to her hotel with a smile. Marissa and Amanda hugged and promised to keep in touch before too long.

Max turned to Marissa as the elevator doors closed and said, "Now we need to have a talk!"

Chapter 30

Marissa convinced Max that they needed to wait a few more weeks before she took a pregnancy test. She explained how, after having been on birth control for so many years, her body would need to get used to being without the hormones. Max understood her rationalization, but was hopeful it was more than that.

They fell into bed at an early hour after such a busy and emotionally draining day. Holding her back against his chest, Max fondled her breasts and plucked her nipples as she questioned him about her concerns with her father's estate. Smiling, he told her that finances would never be an issue for her now. She could give everything away and still always be secure. She reached behind her, stroking his cock as she explained that she wasn't entitled to anything he had since they were not yet married. His response took her by surprise when he said he had already put her name on the penthouse and all of his accounts. She squeezed his erection as she gasped. "Careful honey, or you are going to be wearing my release on your back if you keep doing that!" She giggled as she pushed his back to the mattress while straddling his hips. Mounting his erection, they both moaned, and she rode him fast and hard. "Oh my God, cowgirl! This stallion is ready to blow!" Purring through her own walls, contracting brought them both the release they were chasing! Flopping on his chest, panting, she asked when he put her name on everything. He laughed at her husky-voiced question and told her as soon as they got engaged, he took care of making sure she would always be secure. "Life is never certain, and now you and all of our babies will always be taken care of."

Snuggling into his side with her head on his chest, listening to that heartbeat that always soothed her, they both drifted off.

Waking to the text from her sister saying goodbye for now brought a smile to her face. She ducked under the covers and woke Max with her tongue and hand, massaging him expertly. Living this life made her so happy she wanted to be sure to thank him regularly!

Groaning as he blew down her throat, he asked what made him the lucky recipient of that wake-up blow job. She told him this would be her wake-up call whenever he wanted it. "Beats any alarm I've ever had!" was the last thing he said as he took her mouth in a deep, sensuous kiss.

SEVERAL WEEKS LATER

Marissa dove from the bed as her stomach lurched at sunrise. Laughing, Max asked if he should have the OBGYN come for a house call. He hopped up to hold her hair as she emptied anything left in her stomach. She claimed that it was the food they had been eating recently, declaring that the rich food just wasn't sitting well. He grabbed her by both hands to help her to her feet and looked her in the eye as he told her that her denial was amazing. "It has been how long since you have had a period?" Palming her breast, he said, "And these don't hurt at all?" She shrugged and said, "Maybe." He smiled and pulled her to his chest as he said, "I don't think we even need a test at this point! But having the doctor come and check you out may make sense."

Only Max's money could have an obstetrician and his nurse, along with some very expensive equipment, come to them. As the doctor took measurements from the internal sonogram, he smiled and declared that Marissa was right around 10 weeks pregnant and should have been on prenatal vitamins for some time already. All she came back with was, "OOPS!" He gave her some pointers on eating small meals frequently: no alcohol and plenty of rest. He called the pharmacy to have the vitamins delivered today.

Once they were alone again, Max couldn't stop grinning as he disrobed her to take her back to bed. Kissing her stomach, he kept moving around her very sensitive body, stroking, kissing and massaging until she couldn't take all of the attention any more. She turned on her side and palmed him while she growled, "Inside now! Pregnancy makes me horny!" Laughing, Max asked what was wrong with that. "I will have to keep you knocked up constantly if that is the side effect!" She grabbed his balls and grinned, stating, "One baby at a time, or these will need some extra attention." He told her that they could keep going forever since money and help would never be an issue. With that, he plunged into her from behind while thrumming her extremely sensitive little bundle of nerves, making her purr.

Hours later, Lionel called, which was unusual nowadays. When Max answered the call, Lionel told him to turn on the TV and watch the press conference. The head of the local office of the FBI was on the screen talking about the efforts of the FBI, Interpol, and DEA in bringing down a far-reaching Sex-slave trade and Arms network. Lionel was in the background, grinning from ear to ear. There were quite a number of notorious names, and government higher-ups that have been arrested. Explaining that this network spanned across the U.S., Central America, South America, and at least six European countries. He explained that there had been a number of citizens here in D.C. who were instrumental in the takedown. Names will not be disclosed for the safety of those people. As the T.V. personalities for that channel came on to pontificate, Max turned the T.V. off. Hugging and kissing Marissa, Max announced that they could finally make plans for their wedding.

Looking online to find the perfect location, they spent hours until actually bleary-eyed. Marissa requested someplace warm and sandy. Smiling, she said she didn't even want to wear shoes. There were so many options on islands in the Caribbean or the Pacific. Max then reminded her that they needed to do it relatively soon if she wanted to travel before her last trimester. He then asked if she wanted to do it before she was showing too much. Her response was, "I'm not trying to impress anyone. This is for us and an intimate group of friends only." making him smile broadly. He had an idea in the back of his mind of leasing an entire island for a week to host their closest friends. The only thing that had to be taken into account was the seasonal storms.

Marissa was now scrolling through online sites for soft summer dresses. She wanted something in an empire design made from ivory diaphanous fabric to blow in the coastal breezes. Imagining the fabric catching on her baby bump made her smile. She pictured Max in ivory linen pants and a shirt with a warm tan on his gorgeous body. She knew she would have to choose between her sister and best friend to stand with her. Deep down, she knew Maggie would be the top contender since she had been her bestie for so long!

Musing that all this dreaming was making her hungry, she realized this was the first time in at least six weeks she had been thinking of food without turning green. Catching Max's expression in her periphery, she asked him what diabolical plan was making him look at her in that way. He laughed and said he just loved watching her dream and plan.

Moving over to plant herself on his lap, she grabbed his face and told him she never expected to ever be this happy! Kissing him deeply, she moaned as he palmed her breast and ran his other hand up her leg. Feeling him grow hard under her thigh, she took his hand to lead him to the gym where the St Andrews Cross was at their disposal. Laughing while quickly undressing each other, she reminded him that they would soon be able to go somewhere besides the many rooms they had christened here at the penthouse. Reminding her that they still had one or two surfaces they hadn't yet conquered before they moved on to other places, he smirked and pushed her back to the desired equipment and strapped her on its spread eagle.

Chapter 31

Flying to a mystery island by chopper after their flight to Belize had Marissa smiling to herself and more excited than she had ever felt. Max kept the destination a surprise for her. When they touched down on Ambergris Caye, he explained that he rented the entire resort for their wedding week. They would enjoy and share the pampered seclusion with the guests who were already here in their private villas. Tonight would be a 5-course dinner on the beach for everyone. Tomorrow, those who chose to participate would go out deep sea fishing on the chartered boat. Anyone not interested in fishing could enjoy a leisurely sail on the resort catamaran. On the day of the wedding, guests would be offered a spa day. Each villa had its own private pool for the enjoyment of its occupants. All meals would be catered from the menus left in the villas and served at the occupants' pleasure.

On the third day, after their spa experience, there would be a sunset wedding on the pristine beach. The wedding guests that took the time off to celebrate with Max and Marissa were Roger as best man and Maggie as maid of honor, who not surprisingly opted to share the villa with Roger. FBI agents Lionel, Tim, Abe and Jennifer took vacation time to attend, too. Marissa's sister Amanda was flown in from England. Janet Mayfield, Mark

Winslow and Lanie (Marissa's Therapist) completed the guest list.

Max had someone flown in on the wedding day to do Marissa's hair and makeup. He wanted to be sure she was pampered and relaxed while at the resort. He even set up a special maternity massage therapist to come to their villa the morning of the wedding.

The few days with the guests were a decadent experience and a perfect prelude to the ceremony. On the morning of their wedding, Marissa was feeling anxious and excited simultaneously. Sitting in the chair, having her makeup done and her hair blown into simple beachy waves, was the perfect look. Her nails were polished so that her soft pink toes would poke out from under her dress as she walked barefoot on the beach.

She was ready to don her dress when Max came in and told her he had ordered a light snack of fruit and cheese for them to share. He knew she would be anxious and in need of sustenance. They casually ate while sitting on the veranda that surrounded their pool. When finished, Max took her hand, and they walked to the bedroom where their clothes were laid out on the huge oversized bed. He reluctantly helped her with her dress which was soft layers of diaphanous ivory fabric with a halter neckline that required her to go braless. A soft satin ribbon was tied below her voluptuous breasts, accentuating her visible baby bump. Max groaned, seeing her in nothing but a white lace thong before pulling the dress over her head. He helped her put the finishing touch on—an orchid pinned in her hair behind her right ear.

Marissa then helped Max with his ivory linen shirt. She told him to wait a moment as she retrieved a small box from her makeup case. She handed him the box, which contained the gold, engraved cufflinks she had Maggie pick up for her. The engraving was a large C in the centre with the date of their wedding in a curved design below the initial. Max was delighted with them and pulled her into a tight embrace holding her butt in his hands as he devoured her mouth. Giggling, she said, "You got the baby excited with that kiss. Can you feel him kicking and tumbling?"

After putting themselves back together, they walked to the beach hand in hand. As they stood on the crest of the dune, Marissa gasped in awe. The sky was horizontal ribbons in shades of pink, purple and orange above the aqua waves breaking gently on the shore. The gazebo where they would say their vows was illuminated with strings of fairy lights and adorned with fragrant blossoms. Barefoot, they stepped up onto the gazebo floor from the soft white sands.

Max never let go of her hands the entire time they said their vows. It was almost as if he expected her to disappear if he relinquished his hold. Just as they were ready to seal their marriage with the kiss, a helicopter descended onto the beach nearby, grabbing everyone's attention. As the rotors stopped spinning, a white-haired gentleman stepped off and walked toward them. Marissa almost fainted, seeing who it was. She and Amanda gasped and whispered, "Papa? How is this possible?" He stopped in front of Marissa and Max and said, "I didn't want to miss my daughter's wedding!" Marissa spoke from behind, her hands covering her mouth in shock as she gasped again, saying, "But you're dead. How is this possible?" Laughing, Malcolm Calloway the 3rd bellowed, "Money can even buy a substitute that can pass as me after extensive plastic surgery! Now give me a hug, baby girl, and introduce me to your husband!"

Printed in Great Britain
by Amazon